PRAIRIE STATE BOOKS

	DATE DUE	
MAR 29 2008		

In conjunction with the Illinois Center for the Book, the
University of Illinois Press is reissuing in paperback
works of fiction and nonfiction that are, by virtue
of authorship and/or subject matter, of particular
interest to the general reader in the state of Illinois.

SERIES EDITORS

Michael Anania, University of Illinois at Chicago
Robert Bray, Illinois Wesleyan University
John Hallwas, Western Illinois University
James Hurt, University of Illinois at Urbana-Champaign
Maria Mootry, Grinnell College

BOARD OF ADVISORS

Roger D. Bridges, Illinois Historic Preservation Agency
John Mack Faragher, Mount Holyoke College
George Hendrick, University of Illinois at Urbana-Champaign
Babette Inglehart, Chicago State University
Robert W. Johannsen, University of Illinois at Urbana-Champaign
Bridget L. Lamont, Illinois State Library
Kenneth Nebenzahl, Chicago
Ralph Newman, Chicago
Howard W. Webb, Jr., Southern Illinois University at Carbondale

---

A list of books in the series appears at the end of this volume.

The Valley of Shadows:
Sangamon Sketches

The Valley of Shadows:
Sangamon Sketches

FRANCIS GRIERSON

Introduction by Robert Bray

UNIVERSITY OF ILLINOIS PRESS
Urbana and Chicago

Introduction © 1990 by the Board of Trustees
of the University of Illinois
Manufactured in the United States of America

P 5 4 3 2 1

This book is printed on acid-free paper.

Library of Congress Cataloging-in-Publication Data

Grierson, Francis, 1848–1927.
    [Valley of shadows. Selections]
  The valley of shadows : Sangamon sketches / Francis Grierson :
introduction [and edited] by Robert Bray.
      p.   cm. — (Prairie State books)
  Consists of the first 12 chapters of Valley of shadows.
  Bibliography: p.
  ISBN 0-252-06103-9 (alk. paper)
    1. Illinois—History—1778–1865—Fiction. 2. United States—
History—Civil War, 1861–1865—Fiction. I. Bray, Robert C.
II. Title. III. Series.
PS3513.R658V35   1990
813'.4—dc20   89-20148
                                         CIP

THESE PAGES—CONCERNING ABRAHAM LINCOLN
AND HEROIC TIMES—ARE DEDICATED
TO MY SISTER,

MRS. JOSEPH VANCE

Contents

Introduction

The Prairie State Books edition of Francis Grierson's *Valley of Shadows* marks, as close as I have been able to reckon, only the sixth printing since 1909, the year of first publication. This is a sadly meager publishing history for a book that has been called "unique," "unforgettable," "a masterpiece," and, in the judgment of preeminent critic Bernard DeVoto, an "American classic."[1] Despite such acclaim, however, *The Valley of Shadows* has never been widely read, either in Illinois or the nation, and is today mainly kept alive by a small group of teachers of midwestern regional literature. I number myself among these enthusiasts and hope that a new edition will help gain *The Valley of Shadows* the wider readership and critical consideration it deserves. Yet what readers will find here is more than a new edition; *The Valley of Shadows: Sangamon Sketches* is virtually a new book that includes the preface, "Proem," and the twelve opening chapters—about three-fifths of Grierson's original. While I will be arguing that the cuts enhance rather than compromise literary quality, this is, quantitatively at least, a radical abridgment. I have added the subtitle both to distinguish this edition from its predecessors and to indicate the narrative core that now stands alone as *The Valley of Shadows*.[2]

To abridge in this manner assumes, of course, an editorial license that Grierson didn't grant in his lifetime. Because I knew I might be violating his authorial intention—though his intention is not entirely clear—the decision was very difficult. As an editor, I would not lightly delete any text, let alone more than a hundred pages; nor as a reader would I ever accept such major surgery without sufficient justification. Fortunately, the case for abridging reposes strongly in a crucial recognition, one made by every generation of readers since 1909: *The Valley of Shadows: Sangamon Sketches* is really a book within a book, a story on its own, and far more coherent than the desultory writing that follows and reads like filler—chapters, for instance, on St. Louis society, General Fremont in the West, his cousin Benjamin Grierson's cavalry raid into Mississippi during the Civil War, really a miscellany of autobiography, essay, and history, and not always authentic: Grierson evidently rewrote a number of the pieces from other sources.[3] The twelve chapters of the "Sangamon Sketches," by contrast, form a powerful artistic whole, a sustained and integral "sacred drama" of sin and redemption enacted on the prairies "round about springfield." This is what has moved readers of *The Valley of Shadows,* and often deeply, but that effect is achieved despite the heavy inertial counterweight of the rest of the book.

The Valley of Shadows: Sangamon Sketches unfolds during the late spring, summer, and early autumn of 1858, the portentous year of Donati's great comet and a time of tumultuous religious revival throughout the nation. Chapter 1 shows the folk going sociably to meeting after a winter of isolation, only to have their fellowship riven by a fiery abolitionist sermon that divides the community along pro- and antislavery lines.

Chapter 12 culminates with the grandly apocalyptic autumnal camp meeting scene. In between, the narrative draws a small group of memorable characters, at once individuals and types whose speech and action make a community rather than a scattered rural settlement; places them in a mystical landscape where it seems "as if anything might happen"; and times them both by the agricultural calendar (the rounds of sowing and reaping) and by eternalizing the diurnal through the harvesting of souls at the camp meeting. The action centers on purifying the community's heart, lifting the shadows, and the drama is wonderfully carried along by Grierson's peculiar style: an alternating current of dialogue in thick "backwoods" dialect and a pervasively poetic narration—diffuse, ethereal, unresolved, like the piano improvisations from Grierson's earlier career as a salon musician.[4]

For Francis Grierson became a writer late in life after an eccentric and rootless existence that spanned the globe. Grierson's biography, and especially his musicianship, are beyond my scope here, but a sketch of his life before *The Valley of Shadows* may suggest how this "strange fish," as Van Wyck Brooks called him, came to write his equally strange book. Grierson was born in England in 1848 and given the formidable name of Benjamin Henry Jesse Francis Shepard (Francis Grierson was both a pen name—taken in 1889— and an affirmation of identity: his mother's family name was Grierson, and he was inordinately fond of her Scottish lineage, which he traced back to Robert Grierson, the historical model for Sir Walter Scott's *Redgauntlet*). The Shepards emigrated to Illinois sometime in the early 1850s, living first in Sangamon and then Macoupin counties before moving on to Alton and St. Louis near the end of the decade. Evidently the pioneering experiment failed, so the family returned to England soon after the Civil War. By 1869 young Jesse Shepard was in Paris exhibiting his newly discovered gifts for piano and vocal improvisation—talents he always claimed as his intuitive own, natural and untutored. Whether this was true or merely a part of the assiduously prepared Grierson mask, his playing seems often to have astonished audiences and affected them profoundly (see note four). Twenty years of musical wandering followed this initial Parisian success: sensational performances at courts and salons throughout France, England, Germany, Denmark, Russia; travel and adventure in the western United States; and finally settlement in London where he began a second career as a writer that was to last until his death in 1927. Why Grierson started writing isn't clear. Perhaps the "mystical prodigy" role was growing tiresome by middle age. Or perhaps Grierson wanted to be taken seriously as an artist and an intellectual and saw writing as the most effective way to reach a larger audience. I'm confident that Grierson's turning toward literature reflected his belief that writing flowed from the same creative wellspring as music. Through writing he could make more convincing (because less abstract) those spiritual connections with life and history, between himself and the world, that he valued over everything else. And this is what he attempted in a series of books, mostly collections of highly personal essays leading up to *The Valley of Shadows,* his chief work and, in part at least, a notable instance of one great spirit invoking another: Abraham Lincoln.

Abraham Lincoln's spiritual presence in the "Sangamon Sketches" (he is not actually a character) reminds us that this was his Valley and Garden across which slavery cast its dark and deadly shadow. The folk, no less than Lincoln, were the chosen vessels of transcendent forces: "In the late 'fifties the people of Illinois were being prepared for the new era by a series of scenes and incidents that nothing but the term 'mystical' will fittingly describe."[5] To Grierson's retrospective, idealizing imagination the area round about Springfield was, for a brief period just before the Civil War, a metonymy for the nation. "Sin in politics air ekil te sin in religion—thar ain't no dividin' line," declares the community's "local Lincoln" and "Load-Bearer," Elihu Gest, in what is surely the signal theme of Grierson's American allegory (69).

Elihu Gest and his ilk practice what they preach while walking through the valley of the shadow of death, risking their lives to conduct the Underground Railroad and earnestly searching nature for symbolic tokens of right action. The best of them (Kezia Jordan, Zack Caverly, Isaac Snedeker—all quaintly named) seem finally to triumph over time and slavery and their own troubled selves, though at a terrific cost: "The year of jubilee has come, / Return ye ransomed sinners home" sing thousands in unison on the camp meeting's "night of nights," and this just after blameless Kezia Jordan's blameless son Alek has been killed by a bolt of lightning from unaccountable providence. As the Load-Bearer watches the swaying, surging ocean of humanity on the campground, watches the dance of redemption inspired by the hurricane-force winds of his preaching, he pronounces the last words of the "Sangamon Sketches," not quite a warning, not quite benediction: "'Let 'em mourn, let 'em mourn' jedgment ain't far off!'" (153).

If 1858 wasn't after all the "year of jubilee," it was at least a profound presentiment of the Civil War soon to come.

In what may serve as a brief epilogue to the "Sangamon Sketches," Grierson shows us the Load-Bearer one last time. Like Walt Whitman, he had gone south to serve as a nurse, returning home after the fall of Vicksburg, broken in body if not in spirit: "[A]s I was roaming about the [Alton] levee, I saw a steamboat arrive and some of the passengers come ashore. Among them was a man who was hardly able to walk and who stopped to look about him as if in search of someone. In a few moments a woman came running down to meet him. The man was Elihu Gest, the Load-Bearer, so changed by illness that at first I did not know him."[6]

Oddly, we never learn whether Elihu Gest lives and goes back to his homestead or dies, like his beloved Lincoln, a casualty of the holocaust. But we sense that his time as communal load-bearer is in any case done.

Such a précis of the action cannot begin to convey the strange and memorable beauty of the narrative, which I encourage readers to discover for themselves. I know that until I read the "Sangamon Sketches" as a single action I didn't realize what kind of literature *The Valley of Shadows* is and has always been: formed fiction. Probably I was misled by Grierson's own declaration of genre in the preface: "This book is not a novel, but the recollections of scenes and episodes of my early life in Illinois" (ix). Grierson announces a memoir of childhood, a long "labour of love" written from his residence in England over a ten-year period, a fond remembrance of a time and a place long ago and far away, filtered through the nostalgic double vision of Grierson the man and his boy persona. Romanticized memory, to be sure, but no less *recollections,* he insisted, for such coloration. The things of the book were things that once had happened to Francis Grierson. Now, in narrative, he was making them happen again.

The world, by and large, has taken him at his word. Librarians classify *The Valley of Shadows* as history; historians, without blinking, sometimes read and use the book as if it were an eyewitness account of events in Lincolnland during the 1850s. And they have often found the evocative, poetic style a pleasant surprise, the more impressive for being unexpected and at the service, so they thought, of a nonfiction subject and literary form. Bernard DeVoto, who was an esteemed historian and critic, took this view in his editor's note to the 1948 History Book Club edition. He particularly admired the vividness and authenticity of the opening scene in which the Reverend Azariah James preaches the first real abolitionist sermon the prairie community has ever heard: "We must remember that this is not a scene in fiction; it is a laboriously crystallized memory of something seen and heard. So with everything else in the book." Thus did the historian in DeVoto persuade the critic. He concluded that *The Valley of Shadows* was in fact *better* than a novel because it had the "immediateness of fiction" but the "substance of actuality."[7] DeVoto may unconsciously have compared Grierson to Mark Twain: the artistry of both, he suggests, was founded on the same "laboriously crystallized memory." Twain reputedly had nearly total recall, at least of Hannibal, and DeVoto had assiduously studied the process by which memory became literary art in *Mark Twain at Work* (1942). Without picking a quarrel with DeVoto, I believe he widely misunderstands fictive forms and their differences (if any) from nonfiction. Twain himself burlesqued this very actualizing power of memory in a famous passage from his *Autobiography:* "When I was younger I could remember anything, whether it had happened or not; but my faculties are decaying now, and soon I shall be so I cannot remember any but the things that never happened."[8] Grierson, I should note, was certainly of the temperament to "remember what didn't happen"—and getting along toward the age, too. Similarly, a remark I once heard Wright Morris make about his art is apposite here: "Memory processed by emotion *is* fiction." But the real problem is that DeVoto didn't look as closely at Grierson as he had Twain. He read and appreciated the text of *The Valley of Shadows,* but without much attention to context, and none to "intertext": books are about books as much as they're about anything else, and DeVoto failed to notice the occasional clue that Grierson gives to his reading.

As we've seen, Grierson called the writing of *The Valley of Shadows* a "labour of love." "It took me ten years to write," he later claimed, "and all my fortune to the *last* silver shilling. When the last page was finished, the last shilling was spent."[9] Why would it take so long to write a 278-page book (in large type at that)? And what was he doing during these years of totalizing work? DeVoto notwithstanding, surely more than trying hard to remember and even more than "polishing every sentence," as Edmund Wilson put it, "with a solicitude that was almost Flaubertian."[10] Much of his time, I suspect, Grierson spent intensively reading and researching the American 1850s. We can safely assume that he continued to feed his fixed fascination with Lincoln, a subject he returned to time and again. But *The Valley of Shadows* reveals little of its sources (the only title directly mentioned is Stowe's *Uncle Tom's Cabin,* which for Grierson was a book like his own, written under a "compelling influence" and illuminating its times). Grierson covers his traces well, yet occasionally a faint trail is discernible. For example, John Hallwas has shown that Chapters 13–14, "The Pioneer of Sangamon County" and "The Regulators," are a redaction of a tale previously printed in John L. McConnell's *Western Characters* (1853).[11] And within the narrative territory of the "Sangamon Sketches" an obvious (though uncredited) source is Peter Cartwright's *Autobiography* (1856).

Like Lincoln, Cartwright is frequently alluded to in the "Sangamon Sketches" though kept offstage. Unquestionably, the old Methodist circuit preacher—he would have been seventy-three in 1858—was a mighty presence in Sangamon County when Grierson and his family lived there. By that time his legendary status had been building for more than thirty years, so the boy narrator might plausibly have heard Cartwright tales from his neighbors or even attended one of his celebrated meetings. But more likely he remembered the legend and went to the *Autobiography* (also a best-seller in the late 1850s, though not in the blockbuster class of Stowe's novel) for material. Like so many others before and since, Grierson couldn't resist using some of Cartwright's best stories.

Briefly looking at two of them adapted for *The Valley of Shadows* can help us understand Grierson's fictionalizing imagination. First, the well-known General Jackson incident as told by the Load-Bearer:

"Old Hickory I see oncet at a Methodist meetin'. Pete Cartwright war a-preachin' when Old Hickory walked in. The presidin' elder sez te the preacher: 'Thet's Andrew Jackson'; but Pete Cartwright didn't noways keer. 'Who's Andrew Jackson?' he sez. 'If he's a sinner God'll damn him the same as He would a Guinea nigger'" (70). [12]

The *Autobiography* recounts this incident as having occurred in Nashville, Tennessee, in 1819. If born at all, Elihu Gest would have been too young if he had been there. [13] And "Elihu Gest" is probably a fictional name for a fictional character—no such person survives in the biographical records of Sangamon, Morgan, or Macoupin counties, and the name itself is an allegorical pun: "Elihu" (in Hebrew "he is God") + "G(u)est" = a temporary redeemer among the Illinois host. Because the General Jackson story is so good, I've made a determined effort to trace it to either an oral source or a printed version before the *Autobiography,* but there is none. Cartwright himself probably promulgated the story in 1856, from which point it spread and became legendary (whether it is true or not is another matter).

The other Cartwright story figures more intricately in Grierson's narrative. The teller this time is Serena Busby, a good-natured gossip given to tales that I suspect have their origins in "old southwestern humor," which is where Cartwright had picked up his own linguistic trappings. After regaling the boy and his family with an account of "chivareeing"—the country custom of playing of practical jokes on just-married couples—she recollects a story about Jack Haywood and his new wife, "widder Brown:"

"His fust wife druv him te drinkin' en this one druv him te religion. He got converted, but fust off she wus dead set agin preachers, en scuffled up agin preachin' en prayin' in dead earnest till Haywood was most druv crazy. When Pete Cartwright come 'long one day he says she stormed en raved used cuss words, en when he said he wus goin' te pray right in the cabin she shook her fist in his face en 'lowed she wus one half alligator en t'other half snappin' turtle, en dared him te put her out, ez he said he would if she didn't behave; she said it 'ud take a better man than he wus te do it" (114).

Sure enough, Cartwright locks her out of her own house, and the story goes on for two more pages to its predictable end: the woman humbled, contrite, religiously awakened. Grierson takes the incident directly from Cartwright (*Autobiography*, 305 – 7), but makes his own through the comic characterization and dialect. Mrs. Busby ends the chapter with yet another story—her fourth in a row—and this one palpably of the "humorous sketch" variety so popular in antebellum newspapers throughout the West. It concerns a stubborn and misfortunate woman named Almedy Sinclair who tries to ride an unrideable "chesnut" at the county fair horse races and ends up thrown, "'settin' like a sack o' seed pertaters while t'other gal rid by on her prancin' roan ez big ez life en twicet ez sassy'" (117). Does this sound like something Grierson heard as a boy and remembered, or something he read as a man and rewrote?

Ironically, this particular scene of storytelling recently caught the interest of John Mack Faragher in his important book *Sugar Creek,* a detailed social history of a single frontier community in southern Sangamon County, 1817 to the Civil War. *The Valley of Shadows* provides Faragher with some important evidence, but of what? Like DeVoto, he treats the book as a species of nonfiction. Stories like chivareeing and

Jack Haywood, both of which he highlights, are read as revealing of local frontier folkways, and especially the attitudes
and roles of the pioneer women of Sugar Creek. But what if
they didn't live in the community? What if they never existed
at all? "Francis Grierson wrote," or "Francis Grierson told a
story," Faragher begins, yet does not go on to say that the
quoted information is typical rather than actual, or that it
derives from a literary context, words put in the mouth of a
fictional character who is not so much reporting experience as
telling jokes, complete with punch lines, some of them as old
as the Virginia and Kentucky hills from which they came.
This is not to say that literary evidence is inadmissible, in
historical argument or anywhere else, only that it must be
recognized as such—as applying to wider, often universal, human circumstances and not to the microcosm of community
along Sugar Creek south of Springfield.[14]

What is "actual" in the narrative is hard to isolate. Young
Francis Grierson did indeed live with his family round about
Springfield during the epiphanic year of 1858, and presum-
ably he witnessed or heard of some of the events that made
their way into the "Sangamon Sketches." A few of the characters are based on historical models, the best example being
the intrepid engineer of the Underground Railroad, Isaac
Snedeker, whose local reputation as "a total stranger to fear"
became legendary in Morgan County.[15] But, once again,
whether Grierson was remembering or reading (or both) is
problematic.

If we may be sure of anything, it is that Grierson relied on
the interfusing power of his romantic imagination to join experience and documentation into a compelling narrative of
the Illinois Garden—pristine, threatened, redeemed, and

transformed into a new "Canaan," as Harold Simonson has described the symbolic progress of the narrative.[16] The mystical landscape of *The Valley of Shadows* is both beautiful and sublime, by turns redolent and obscure, idyllic and apocalyptic. Edmund Wilson in *Patriotic Gore* likewise perceived that the book was a "sacred drama," and he was struck by the atmosphere and the artistry behind it: "The landscapes as seen by a child, the special sensations of night and day, moonrise and sunset, winter and summer, in a lonely log cabin beyond civilization, are created with all the skill that a high civilization can teach; and the rude people on their little farms are differentiated and understood with a cultivated sensitivity that never patronizes them."[17]

And, in a letter dated 23 August 1911, another writer and Illinois expatriate, Mary Austin, paid the most moving tribute to Grierson's book I've ever read: "Often, while I have read your book, I would lay it aside and weep quietly for I knew not what. . . . It was as if something—the spirit of the land, perhaps—which I had worshipped afar off, had turned back after all these years and hailed me."[18]

John Hallwas has cogently argued that the "Sangamon Sketches" are precisely the novel Grierson denied the *entire* book was; he has further speculated that Grierson wrote the first twelve chapters at an earlier time and may even have intended them as a "short novel."[19] Hallwas's careful analysis shores up my own intuition about the book and helps complete the justification for abridging it. But whatever the genre, *The Valley of Shadows* is high-order fiction. In a sense, the "not a novel" disclaimer may be partly owing to the author's disgust with the dominant literary realism of his age. He detested French and American naturalism, Zola and his *bête humaine,* and the tedious heaping of social detail to no evident purpose other than making what he called "a crude and sodden mass" of unleavened narrative for the popular market—no yeast, no expanse, and certainly no book of his.[20] What Grierson sought in his own writing was the illusion of the ideal as immanent in the world, and to this sort of late-Romantic program the doctrines of realism were a definite hindrance—something to be reacted against. Grierson didn't mind constituting a majority of one, yet he knew what he was up against: "[B]ooks like mine are not, and never will be written for money," he wrote, not regretting either the money he had spent on *The Valley of Shadows* or the money he wasn't going to make from it. His book was for himself, for history and the future. He took the long view because he was, he didn't scruple saying, a genius: "*The Valley of Shadows* had to be written by me, or not written at all. The fundamental reasons & conditions of that time had to be recorded in that *particular* form. . . . The art that is not felt is not art at all, but something else. Genius is self-conscious or it is nothing."[21] The emphasis on *particular* is his: the apparently amorphous book had its form, a form specifically embodying the genius of Francis Grierson, who self-consciously made the narrative the way it had to be.

NOTES

1. Theodore Spencer, in his introductory essay to the History Book Club edition, calls *The Valley of Shadows* "a minor classic of American literature." DeVoto goes him one better: "I should be willing to delete the adjective." Francis Grierson, *The Valley of Shadows,* ed. Theodore Spencer (New York: History

Book Club, 1948), ix, xviii. The previous printings I have been able to identify are as follows: the first English edition (1909); the first American edition (1909); the second English edition (1913); the History Book Club edition (1948); the College and University Press edition (1970); and, most recently, the inclusion of the first twelve chapters in John Hallwas's *Illinois Literature: The Nineteenth Century* (Macomb: Illinois Heritage Press, 1986).

2. "Sangamon Sketches" not so much in the sense of the Sangamon River, which plays no part in the narrative, but the area "round about Springfield" that long went by the name "Sangamo Country."

3. John Hallwas, "The Problem of Unity in *The Valley of Shadows*," *MidAmerica* 8 (1981): 51.

4. Under his real name, Jesse Shepard, Grierson made a remarkable career as a musician in Europe. Granted, there was always "a touch of the charlatan" in him, as Van Wyck Brooks remembered in *Scenes and Portraits* (New York: E. P. Dutton, 1954), 231, and the foolish trappings of spiritualism and theosophy gave his musicales an air that skeptics thought meretricious. Yet Mallarmé called him "the first real poet of the piano," and the other-worldliness of his playing, as reported by those who heard it, must have sounded like the poetic effects of some of the best scenes in *The Valley of Shadows* (the "Log-House" chapter springs immediately to mind). Here is Edwin Bjorkman trying to describe the indescribable, one of Grierson's performances: "It opened with a procession of chords—haunting, monotonous, primitive. It was as if the horns and drums of some African village had become civilized without losing their original weirdness—as if their uncouth noises had become miraculously transformed into genuine harmonies while still echoing the strife of primeval passions. Something more than sound issued from that piano: it was a mood "uncanny," yet pleasing, exalting, luring." "The Music of Francis Grierson," *Harper's Weekly* 58 (14 Feb. 1914): 15.

5. Francis Grierson, *The Valley of Shadows* (Urbana: University of Illinois Press, 1990), 1 (all parenthetical page references are to this edition).

6. Francis Grierson, *The Valley of Shadows* (Boston: Houghton, Mifflin Co., 1909), 277.

7. Spencer, xiii-xiv.

8. Albert Bigelow Paine, ed., *Mark Twain's Autobiography* (New York: Harper and Brothers, 1924), 1, 96.

9. As quoted in Spencer, xxxii.

10. Edmund Wilson, *Patriotic Gore* (New York: Oxford University Press, 1962), 78.

11. Hallwas, 51.

12. The General Jackson story occurs in Peter Cartwright, *Autobiography* (New York: Nelson and Phillips, 1856), 192. Perhaps it is worth mentioning that Cartwright himself never used the slurring word *nigger* in either the manuscript or the text of his *Autobiography*. He might have been expected to use it in speech, however, and certainly oral tradition would have no hesitation in the matter, which might give some slight credence to the notion of an oral source for Grierson. On the other hand, nowhere in print have I seen Cartwright called "Pete"—the references are always to Peter or Uncle Peter—which suggests that Grierson was familiar with him at second or third hand.

13. No exact age for Elihu Gest is given in the narrative, and as Load-Bearer he seems appropriately ageless. Nevertheless, on page 26 he says to the boy's mother, "I've been nigh on thirty year wrastlin' with the sorrows o'life.'" If this refers to his actual age, then he obviously couldn't have witnessed the General Jackson scene.

14. John Mack Faragher, *Sugar Creek* (New Haven: Yale University Press, 1986), 116–17.

15. Hallwas, 55.

16. Harold Simonson, *Francis Grierson* (New York: Twayne, 1966), 111–19. Simonson's interpretation differs from John Hallwas's (and mine) in attempting to make a case for the unity of the entirety of Grierson's original.

17. Wilson, 79.

18. As quoted in Simonson, 107.

19. Hallwas, 55–56. For a study of the symbolic unity of the sacred drama in *The Valley of Shadows* see Robert Bray, "The Mystical Landscape: Francis Grierson's *The Valley of Shadows*," *The Old Northwest* 5, no. 4 (1979): 367–85; and *Rediscoveries: Literature and Place in Illinois* (Urbana: University of Illinois Press, 1982), 35–51.

20. Grierson's judgment of the realistic novel is worth quoting in full: "[It] can be produced by one or more persons in every town. The facts are there before you—marriages, births, divorces, feasts, and funerals; knead them, like dough for a dumpling, season the lump with the spice of passion, and the crude and sodden mass is ready for the market." In *Modern Mysticism* (London: Stephen Swift, 1911), 128.

21. As quoted in Spencer, xxxii–xxxiii.

Preface

This book is not a novel, but the recollections of scenes and episodes of my early life in Illinois and Missouri, the writing of which has been a labour of love. A cosmopolitan life in the different capitals of Europe during a period of forty years has not sufficed to alienate the romance and memory of those wonderful times.

In looking back I have come to the conclusion that the power displayed by the most influential preachers and politicians of the *ante-bellum* days in Illinois was a power emanating from the spiritual side of life, and I have done my best to depict the "silences" that belonged to the prairies, for out of those silences came the voices of preacher and prophet and a host of workers and heroes in the great War of Secession.

In 1863 President Lincoln issued his famous proclamation for the emancipation of the slaves, and with it the old order passed away never to return. Indeed, the social upheaval of that year was greater than that produced by the Declaration of Independence in 1776, and no matter what happens now, the old political and social conditions can never be revived. Not only have the people changed, but the whole face of the nation has changed—the prairies are gone, and luxurious homes are to be found in the places where log-houses, primitive woods, and wild flowers were the only prominent features of the landscape for many miles together.

I have recorded my impressions of the passing of the old democracy and the old social system in the United States, and, curiously enough, I witnessed again in 1869-70, while residing in Paris, the passing of another social order—that of Napoleon and the Empire, the recollections of which I shall leave for a future volume.

F. G.

Mill House, Radclive, Buckingham.
January, 1909.

Proem

IN THE late 'Fifties the people of Illinois were being prepared for the new era by a series of scenes and incidents which nothing but the term "mystical" will fittingly describe.

Things came about not so much by preconceived method as by an impelling impulse. The appearance of "Uncle Tom's Cabin" was not a reason, but an illumination; the founding of the Republican party was not an act of political wire-pulling, but an inspiration; the great religious revivals and the appearance of two comets were not regarded as coincidences, but accepted as signs of divine preparation and warning.

The settlers were hard at work with axe and plough; yet, in spite of material pre-occupation, all felt the unnameable influence of unfolding destiny. The social cycle, which began with the Declaration of Independence, was drawing to a close, and during Buchanan's administration the collective consciousness of men—that wonderful prescience of the national soul—became aware of impending innovation and upheaval.

It was impossible to tell what a day might bring forth. The morning usually began with new hope and courage; but the evening brought back the old silences, with the old, unsolved questionings, strange presentiments, premonitions, sudden alarms. Yet over and around all a kind of sub-conscious humour welled up, which kept the *mind hopeful while the heart was weary. Dressed in butter-nut jeans, and swinging idly on a gate, many a youth of the time might have been pointed out as a likely Senator, poet, general, ambassador, or even President. Never was there more romance in a new country. A great change was coming over the people of the West. They retained all the best characteristics of the Puritans and the settlers of Maryland and Virginia, with something strangely original and characteristic of the time and place, something biblical applied to the circumstances of the hour.*

Swiftly and silently came the mighty influences. Thousands laboured on in silence; thousands were acting under an imperative, spiritual impulse without knowing it; the whole country round about Springfield was being illuminated by the genius of one man, Abraham Lincoln, whose influence penetrated all hearts, creeds, parties, and institutions.

People were attracted to this region from Kentucky, Missouri, Indiana, the shores of the Ohio, the British Isles, France, and Germany. Other States had their special attractions: Indiana, Kentucky, and Missouri contained hills and forests appealing to the eye by a large and generous variation of landscape; Iowa and Kansas sloped upward toward the West, giving to the mind an ever-increasing sense of hope and power. To many, Illinois seemed the last and the least because the most level. Only a poet could feel the charm of her prairies, only a far-seeing statesman could predict her future greatness.

The prairie was a region of expectant watchfulness, and life a perpetual contrast of work and idleness, hope and misgiving. Across its bosom came the covered wagons with their human freight, arriving or departing like ships between the shores of strange, mysterious worlds.

The early Jesuit missionaries often spoke of the Illinois prairie as a sea of grass and flowers. A breeze springs up from the shores of old Kentucky, or from across the Mississippi and the plains of Kansas, gathering force as the hours steal on, gradually changing the aspect of Nature by an undulating motion of the grass, until the breeze has become a gale, and behold the prairie a rolling sea! The pennant-like blades dip before the storm in low, rushing billows as of myriads of green birds skimming the surface. The grassy blades bend to the rhythm of Nature's music, and when clouds begin to fleck the far horizon with dim, shifting vapours, shadows as of long grey wings swoop down over the prairie, while here and there immense fleeting veils rise and fall and sweep on towards the sky-line in a vague world of mystery and illusion.

The prairies possessed a charm created by beauty instead of awe; for besides the countless wild flowers they had rivers, creeks, lakes, groves, and wooded strips of country bordering the large streams.

Everywhere, even in the most desolate places, at all times and seasons, signs of life were manifest in the traces, flights, and sounds of animals and birds. Over the snow, when all seemed obliterated, appeared the track of the mink, fox, and chick-a-dee, while during the greater part of the year the grass, woods, and air were alive with winged creatures that came and went in a perpetual chorus of audible or inaudible song.

The prairie was an inspiration, the humble settlers an ever-increasing revelation of human patience and progress. There was a charm in their mode of living, and real romance in all the incidents and events of that wonderful time.

Chapter I

The Meeting-House

ALL through the winter the meeting-house on Saul's Prairie had stood deserted and dormant, its windows rattling in the bleak winds, perhaps longing for the coming revivals and the living, vital sympathy of beings "clothed in garments divine"; but now, how different it looked on this wonderful Sunday morning, with its door and windows wide open, the flowers in bloom, and the birds perched on the tallest weeds pouring forth their song! The fleckless sky and soft, genial atmosphere had made of the desolate little meeting-house and its surroundings a place that resembled a second Garden of Eden.

How calm and beautiful was the face of Nature! The prairie here in Illinois, in the heart of Lincoln's country, had a spirit of its own, unlike that of the forest, and I had come to look upon the meeting-house as a place possessing a sort of soul, a personality which made it stand out in my imagination as being unique among all the meeting-houses I had ever seen. It must, I thought, feel the states of the weather and the moods of the people.

The settlers made their way to meeting in wagons, on horseback, and on foot; and for nearly an hour people straggled in. They came in family groups, and a moment of excitement would be followed by a period of impatient waiting. They came from the west, where a faint column of smoke rose in a zigzag in the warm, limpid atmosphere; from the north, where houses and cabins were hidden in groves or in hollows; from the south, where a forest of old oaks and elms bordered the horizon with a belt of dark green; and from the east, where the rolling prairie spread beyond the limits of vision, a far-reaching vista of grass and flowers.

I had arrived early on my pony. Our neighbours would be here, and I should see some of them for the first time.

Silas Jordan and his wife, Kezia, were among the first to arrive. He, small, thin, and shrivelled, with wiry hair and restless nerves, had a face resembling a spider's web; cross-bars of crows' feet encircled two small, ferret-like eyes, sunk deep in their sockets, out of which he peered with eager suspicion at the moving phenomena of the world. She, with that deep glow that belongs to the dusk of certain days in autumn, had jet-black hair, smoothed down till it covered the tops of her ears; her neck rose in a column from between two drooping shoulders, and her great lustrous eyes looked out on the world and the people like stars from a saffron sunset. Dark and dreamy, she seemed a living emblem of the tall, dark flowers and the willows that bordered the winding rivers and creeks of the prairies.

Then came the Busbys on a horse that "carried double," Serena Busby wearing a new pink calico dress and sunbonnet, the colour clashing with her reddish hair and freckled face.

When these had settled in their seats there came one of those half-unearthly spells of silence and waiting not unlike those moments at a funeral just before the mourners and the minister make their appearance.

I had taken a seat inside for a while, but I slipped out again just in time to see a man come loping along on a small, shaggy horse, man and animal looking as if they had both grown up on the prairie together. It was Zack Caverly, nicknamed Socrates. Zack was indeed a Socrates of the prairie as well in looks as in speech, and the person who first called him after the immortal sage had one of those flashes of inspiration that come now and then to the cosmopolitan whose experience permits him to judge men by a single phrase or a gesture. He tied his horse to a hitching-post, then stood at the door waiting to see what new faces would appear at the meeting. Here he met his old acquaintance Silas Jordan.

The talk soon turned to personalities.

"Have ye heared who them folks is down yander in the Log-House?" began Silas, alluding to the new home of my parents.

"They air from the old kintry," Socrates answered, his round eyes blinking in a manner not to be described.

"Kinder stuck up fer these diggin's, I'm thinkin'."

"I 'low they ain't like us folk," was the careless response. "They hed a heap o' hired help whar they come from."

"The Squar tole me hisself what kyounties he hez lived in sense he come from the old kintry. He hez lived in two kyounties in Missouri en in four kyounties in Illinois, and now I reckon it's root hog or die ez fur ez these diggin's goes. It's his second trial on prairie land. He 'lows it'll be the last if things don't plough up jest ez he's sot his mind te havin' 'em. He's a-layin' in with the Abolitionists, and he voted oncet fer Abe Lincoln, en he sez he air ready te do it agin."

Socrates looked down the road, and exclaimed:

"Bless my stars! if thar ain't Elihu Gest! He's got a stranger with him."

When Elihu Gest hitched his horse to the fence Socrates greeted him:

"Howdy, howdy, Brother Gest. I war wonderin' what hed become o' ye. Ain't seen ye in a coon's age."

Elihu Gest was known as the "Load-Bearer." He had earned this nickname by his constant efforts to assume other people's mental and spiritual burdens. The stranger he brought with him was the preacher.

"I war jes' wonderin' ez I come along," said the Load-Bearer, "what the Know-nothin's en sech like air a-goin' te do, seein' ez how Lincoln en Douglas air dividin' the hull yearth a-twixt 'em."

"Providence created the Know-nothin's te fill up the chinks," answered Zack Caverly, "en ye know it don't noways matter *what* ye fill 'em up with."

"I 'low the chinks hez to be filled up somehow," replied the Load-Bearer; "en a log-cabin air a mighty good place te live in when a man's too pore te live in a frame house."

"Thet's it; them thar politicioners like Abe Lincoln en Steve Douglas hev quit livin' in log-cabins, en thar ain't no chinks fer the Know-nothin' party te fill," said Socrates.

He had taken out a big jack-knife and was whittling a stick.

" 'Pears like thar's allers three kyinds o' everything—
thar war the Whigs, the Demicrats, en the Know-nothin's,
en thar air three kyinds o' folks all over this here kintry—
the Methodists, the Hardshells, en them thet's saft at
feedin'-time, plumb open fer vittles en dead shet agin
religion. Ez I war explainin' te Squar Briggs t'other day,
in the heavings thar air the sun, the moon, en the stars;
thet air three kyinds agin. En whar hev ye ever see a
kivered wagin 'thout hosses, critters, en yaller dogs?
The yaller dogs air steppin'-stones te the hosses, the hosses
comin' in right betwixt the varmints en human bein's,
which the Scriptur' sez air jest a leetle below the angels.
But ye'd never guess 'thout a heap o' cute thinkin' thet
a yaller dog could make hisself so kinder useful like ez
wal ez pertickler. Ez fer folks gen'ly, thar air three kyinds
—Yankees, niggers, en white people."

"Ye don't calc'late te reckon niggers ez folks!" ejaculated Silas Jordan.

"They air folks jes like we air," said the Load-Bearer,
"en they hev souls te save. They air bein' called on, but
somehow the slave-owners ain't got no ears fer the call."

"Wal," chimed in Socrates, "I ain't agin th' Abolitionists, en up te now I ain't tuck much int'rest in the argi-
mints fer en aginst. I ain't called on fer te jedge noways."
He looked about him and continued: "They air talkin'
'bout freein' the niggers, but some o' these here settlers
ain't got spunk 'nough te choose thar partner fer a dance,
ner ile 'nough in thar j'ints te bow in a ladies' chain.
Mebbe arter all the niggers air a sight better off 'n we uns
air. They ain't got no stakes in the groun'."

At this point there was a shuffling of feet and spitting. Then his thoughts turned to the past.

"Afore Buchanan's election I hed all the fiddlin' I could do, but when Pete Cartwright come along he skeered 'em, en when the Baptists come they doused 'em in p'isen cold water, en now folks air predictin' the end o' the world by this here comet.* I'll be doggoned if I've drawed the bow oncet sence folks got skeered plumb te thar marrer-bones! T'other night when I heared sunthin' snap I warn't thinkin' o' the fiddle, en when I tuck it down the nex' day jes' te fondle it a leetle fer ole times' sake I see it war the leadin' string; en good, lastin' catgut air skase ez crowin' hens in these 'ere parts."

Silas Jordan, returning to the subject of my parents, remarked:

"I reckon them Britishers at the Log-House 'll hev te roll up en wade in if they want te git on in this here deestric'."

Just then the talk was interrupted by the appearance of the persons in question, and the crowd at the door stared in silence as they walked in. When Silas recovered his wits he continued his remarks:

"She's got on a store bunnit en he's got on a b'iled shirt." To which Socrates replied, without evincing the least surprise:

"Tallest man I've seed in these parts 'cept Abe Lincoln."

There was a pause, during which the two men gazed through the open door at the tall man who had passed in and taken a seat.

* Donati's great comet.

There was something strangely foreign and remote in the impression my parents produced at the meeting. My mother wore a black silk gown and a black bonnet with a veil; the tall, straight figure of my father appeared still taller with his long frock coat and high collar, and his serious face and Roman nose gave him something of a patriarchal look, although he was still in the prime of life. The arrival of the family from the Log-House caused a flutter of curiosity, but when it was seen that the newcomers were devout worshippers the congregation began to settle down to a spirit of religious repose.

It was a heterogeneous gathering: humorists who were unconscious of their humour, mystics who did not understand their strange, far-reaching power, sentimental dreamers who did their best to live down their emotions, old-timers and cosmopolitans with a marvellous admixture of sense and sentiment, political prophets who could foresee events by a sudden, illuminating flash and foretell them in a sudden, pithy sentence. It was a wonderful people, living in a second Canaan, in an age of social change and upheaval, in a period of political and phenomenal wonders.

A vague longing filled the hearts of the worshippers. With the doubts and misgivings of the present, there was a feeling that to-morrow would bring the realisation of all the yearnings and promises, and when the preacher rose and announced that wistful old hymn:

> "In the Christian's home in glory
> There remains a land of rest,"

an instant change was produced in the faces of the people.

Silas Jordan led the singing in a high, shrill voice which descended on the meeting like a cold blast through a broken window, but Uriah Busby, always on the look-out for squalls, neutralised the rasping sounds by his full, melodious waves. His voice gave forth an unctuous security, not unmixed with a good part of Christian gallantry. In it there was something hearty and fraternal; it leavened conditions and persons, and made the strangers feel at home.

If Uriah Busby's singing gave substance to the meeting, that of Kezia Jordan gave expression to its soul. In the second line her voice rose and fell like a wave from the infinite depths, with something almost unearthly in its tones, that seemed to bring forth the yearnings of dead generations and the unfulfilled desires of her pioneer parents.

A voice had been heard from behind the thin veil that separates the two worlds.

My mother felt somewhat timid among so many strangers. As she looked down at the hymn-book in her hands, her brows, slightly elevated, gave to her face an expression of pensive reverence. Kezia Jordan had noticed two things about the newcomer: her wonderful complexion and her delicate hands. Kezia had as yet only glanced at the stranger; had she heard her speak, she would have remembered her voice as an influence going straight to the soul, touching at the heart's secrets without naming them—a voice that enveloped the listener as in a mantle of compassion, with intonations suggestive of unaffected sympathy for all in need of it.

My mother had often heard the old Methodist hymns,

but now for the first time she felt the difference between the music of a trained choir and the effects produced by the singing of one or two persons inspired by the spirit of the time, hour, and place. Never had sacred song so moved her. Kezia Jordan had infused into two lines something which partook of revelation. The words of the hymn, then, were true, and not a mere juggling with sentiment. Here was an untrained singer who by an unconscious effort revealed a truth which came to the listener with the force of inexorable law, for the words, "there remains a land of rest," came as a decree as well as a promise; and my mother now realised what life in the Log-House would be for her.

A glance at the singer confirmed the impression created by her singing. There, in her strange prophetic features, shone the indelible imprints made by the lonely years in the long and silent conflict; there, in Kezia Jordan's eyes, shone the immemorial mementoes of the ages gone, while the expression of her face changed as the memories came and went like shadows of silent wings over still, clear waters.

Prayers had been offered with more or less fervour; and now with awkward demeanour the preacher stood up, his pale face and half-scared expression arousing in the minds of many of the people no little curiosity and some apprehension.

"Brethering and sistering," he began, in a rambling way, "ye hev all heared the rumours thet hez been passed from mouth te mouth pertainin' te the signs and wonders o' these here times. Folks's minds is onsettled. But me en Brother Gest hev been wrastlin' with the Sperrit all night yander at his God-fearin' home; we were wrastlin' fer a tex' fittin' this here time en meetin', en it warn't till sommairs nigh mornin' thet Brother Gest opened the Good Book, en p'intin' his finger, sez: 'I hev found it! Hallelujer!' It war Isaiah, nineteenth chapter, twentieth verse."

Here the preacher opened the Bible. He read slowly, emphasising certain words so that even the most obtuse present might catch something of the meaning.

" 'En it shell be *fer* a sign, en *fer* a witness unto the Lord of Hosts in the land of Egypt: fer they shell cry unto the Lord bekase of the oppressors, en he *shell* send them a saviour, en a *great* one, en he shell deliver them.' "

He stopped a moment to let the congregation muse on the text, and then proceeded:

"It looked like when he put his finger on thet tex' Brother Gest war changed ez in a twinklin', en our watchin' en prayin' war over fer thet night. Brethering, with the findin' o' thet tex' our troubles war gone, en in thar place thar come te our innermost feelin's a boundin' joy sech ez on'y them thet hez faith kin know."

Here he lost himself; then, like a drowning man who clutches at a straw, he seized hold of an old hackneyed text, the first that came into his mind, and continued, regardless of consequences:

"Fer ez the Scriptur' sez, 'What came ye out fer te see? A reed shaken by the wind?' I 'low most o' ye hez plenty reeds if ye're anywhars near a snipe deestric', but I reckon ye ain't troubled much by seein' 'em shake."

He began to regain confidence, and leaving reeds he grappled with the earth and the heavens in periods which carried everybody with him.

"But thar ain't a sinner here, thar ain't no Christian here to-day thet warn't plumb shuck up by thet yearth-quake t'other night thet rocked ye in yer beds like ye were bein' rocked in a skiff in the waves behind one o' them Mississippi stern-wheelers. No, brethering, the Lord hez passed the time when He shakes yer cornfields en yer haystacks by a leetle puff o' wind. He hez opened the roof o' Heaven so ye can all see what's a-comin'. He hez made it so all o' ye, 'cept them thet's blind, kin say truly, *'I hev seen it.'* Under ye the yearth hez been shuck, over ye the stars air beginnin' te shift en wander. A besom o' destruc-tion 'll overtake them thet's on the wrong side in this here fight!"

He eyed the people up and down on each side, and then went on:

"But the tex' says, 'He shell send them a saviour, en a *great* one, en he shell deliver them.' Now it air jest ez plain ez the noonday sun thet the Lord God app'ints His own leaders, en it air jest ez plain thet His ch'ice ain't fell on no shufflin' backslider. Ye kin bet all yer land en yer cattle en yer hosses on this one preposition, en thet is ye cain't git away from fac's by no cross-argiments thet many air called but mighty few air chosen; en thet means thet on'y one man is 'p'inted te lead."

At this there was a visible change in the attitude of many of the listeners.

"What air he a-comin' to?" whispered old Lem Stephens to Uriah Busby.

It was a bold stroke; but Elihu Gest, the Load-Bearer, had won over the preacher to speak out, and he was coming to the main point as fast as an artless art and blunt but effective rhetoric would let him.

He proceeded with his sermon, now bringing the expectant people to the verge of the last period, now letting them slip back as if he were giving them a "breathing spell" to brace them for a still stronger stage in the argument. It was wonderful how this simple preacher, without education or training, managed to keep the interest of the congregation at boiling point for more than an hour before he pronounced the two magical words that would unlock the whole mystery of the discourse. Before him sat old Whigs, Know-nothings, and Democrats, Republicans, militant Abolitionists, and outspoken friends of slave-owners in the South. But the Load-Bearer was there, his eyes riveted on the speaker, every nerve strung to the utmost pitch, assuming by moral compact the actual responsibility of the sermon. If the preacher failed Elihu Gest would assume his loads; if the sermon was a triumph he would share in the preacher's triumph.

As the sermon drew to a close it became evident that by some queer, roundabout way, by some process of reasoning and persuasion that grew upon the people like a spell, they were listening, and had all along been listening, to a philippic against slavery.

At last the preacher's face lost its timorous look. With great vehemence he repeated the last part of his text:

" 'Fer they shell *cry* unto the Lord bekase of the oppressors, en he shell send them a saviour, en a *great* one' "—here he struck the table a violent blow—" 'en he shell *deliver* them!' "

There was a moment of bewilderment and suspense,

during which Lem Stephens was preparing for the worst.
His mouth, usually compressed to a thin, straight slit, was
now stiffened by a bull-dog jaw which he forced forward
till the upper lip had almost disappeared; Minerva
Wagner sat rigid, her mummy-like figure encased in
whalebone wrapped in linsey-woolsey.

The preacher gave them no rest:

"Now right here I want ye all te ask yerselves who it
air thet's a-cryin' fer deliverance. Who air it?" he shouted.
"Why, thar ain't but one people a-cryin' fer deliverance,
en they air the slaves down thar in Egypt!"

The words fell like a muffled blow in the silence. Lem
Stephens sat forward, breathless; Uriah Busby heaved a
long sigh; fire flashed from Mrs. Wagner's grey, faded
eyes; Ebenezer Hicks turned in his seat, his bushy eyebrows lowering to a threatening frown; while the face of
Socrates wore a look of calm and neutral curiosity.

But hardly had the meeting realised the full force of
the last words when the preacher put the final questions:

"En *who* shell deliver them? Do any o' ye know?
Brethering, thar ain't but one human creatur' ekil to it,
en thet air Abraham Lincoln. The Lord hez called him!"

An electrical thrill passed through the meeting. A
subtle, permeating power took possession of the congregation, for the preacher had pronounced the first half of the
name, Abraham, in such a way that it seemed as if the
patriarch of Israel was coming once more in person to lead
the people. An extraordinary influence had been evoked;
a living investment of might and mystery, never at any
time very distant, was now close at hand.

Ebenezer Hicks rose, and casting a fierce glance about

him hurried out; Minerva Wagner sprang from her seat like an automaton suddenly moved by some invisible force, and left the meeting, followed by her two tall, lank sons; Lem Stephens hurried after them, and with each step gave vent to his feelings by a loud thump on the bare floor with his wooden leg. When he got to the door he cast one last withering look at the preacher.

But Uriah Busby's voice rang out loud and sonorous:

> "How tedious and tasteless the hours
> When Jesus no longer I see."

The old hymn was taken up by Kezia Jordan in the next line. Once more her voice filled the meeting-house with golden waves, once more every heart beat in unison, and every soul communed in an indescribable outpouring of religious melody.

The whole congregation was singing now. With Kezia's voice a balm of Gilead came pouring over the troubled waters created by the strange, prophetic, and menacing sermon. The Load-Bearer, with hardly voice enough to speak aloud, was singing; the preacher sang even louder than he had preached; Serena Busby sang as I never heard her sing again; and while those who had left the meeting were about to depart they heard what they would never hear repeated. The opportunity to join hands with the coming power had passed, and as they set out for home they must have been haunted by the matchless magic and simplicity of the words and music, and more than ever would the coming hours seem "tedious and tasteless" to them.

Chapter II

The Load-Bearer

WE HAD been four months in the Log-House, and my mother was just beginning to feel at home when one afternoon, as I was sauntering along the road near the gate, I saw a man on foot coming from the south.

As he approached I noticed that his features had a peculiar cast, his hair was rather long, his movements somewhat slow, and when he arrived in front of the gate he squared about and stopped with a sort of jerk, as if he had been dreaming but was now awake and conscious that this was the place he had come to visit. He peered at the Log-House as though awaiting some interior impulse to move him to further action; then he opened the gate, and, walking through the yard to the front door, rapped lightly.

I had followed him in, and when my mother opened the door and the stranger said, in a listless sort of way, "I jes' called to see how ye're gettin' on," I saw it was Elihu Gest, the Load-Bearer.

My mother thanked him, invited him in, and offered him a chair.

"I 'low ye're not long settled in this 'ere section," he said, taking a seat.

"Not long," she answered; "we are quite settled in the house, but on the farm my husband has so much to do he hardly knows where to begin."

She placed the kettle on the stove for coffee, and busied herself about getting the strange visitor some substantial refreshment. I thought I had never seen a face more inscrutable. He eyed my mother with grave interest, and after a silence that lasted some considerable time he said:

"If yer loads is too heavy jes' cast 'em off; the Lord is willin' en I ain't noways contrary."

Not till now did she realise that this was the man she had heard so much about; but not knowing just what to say, she gave no answer.

As he sat and stared at my mother his presence diffused a mysterious influence. My mind was busy with queries: Who sent him? What are his loads? Why does he take such an interest in my mother? And I thought she must be giving him coffee and eatables the better to enable him to support his loads, whatever they might be. She placed the coffee and other good things on the table and cordially invited the stranger to make himself at home. After pouring out a cup of coffee she sat down with folded hands, her pale face more pensive than usual, making some remarks about the weather and the good prospects for the new settlers.

Elihu Gest sat, a veritable sphinx of the prairie, wrapped in his own meditations. She almost feared that his visit might be a portent of some coming calamity, and that he had come to warn her and help her to gather force and courage for the ordeal.

Yet there was something in his look which inspired confidence and even cheerfulness, and she concluded it was good to have him sitting there. He began to sip his coffee, and at last, as if waking from a reverie, he put the question:

"How air ye feelin' in sperrit?"

"The Lord has been merciful," she replied, the question having come as an immediate challenge to her religious faith and courage.

"Yer coffee is mos' appetizin'," he said, with a slight sniff.

"I am glad you like it, and I hope you are feeling rested, for you seem to have come a long way."

"They's a powerful difference a-twixt a mile and what a man's thinkin'. When yer mind is sot on one thing the distance a-twixt two places ain't much noways."

"Do you always walk?" she asked sympathetically.

"It's accordin' te how the hoss is feelin'. If the beast's anyways contrary he gives a snort, ez much ez te say, 'Mebbe I'll carry ye en mebbe I won't'; but when he snorts and kicks both te oncet thet means he'll kick the hind sights off all creation if I try te ride him. I've seen him when Joshua en his trumpet couldn't git him outen the barn door. I don't believe in workin' dumb critters when their sperrits air droopin'. I'm allers more contented when I'm 'bleeged te walk; en hosses air powerful skase."

"Necessity compels us to do many things that seem impossible, but we learn to accept them as the best things for us. Won't you have some more coffee?"

"Yer coffee *is* mos' appetizin', it is so."

"And won't you eat something?"

"I'm much obleeged, but I don't feel no cravin' fer vittles. Accordin' te Sister Jordan, yer cakes en pies beats all she ever see."

"Mrs. Jordan is a very good woman."

"She is so; I've knowed her from away back."

There came another pause, during which the visitor looked straight before him, lost in thought. Presently he began:

"Thet comet's convicted a good many folks. Ebenezer Hicks war skeered half te death when he see it a-comin', makin' the loads mos' heavy fer his pore wife."

Then, addressing my mother, he continued:

"The night he war 'flicted, I couldn't git te sleep nohow. I sez to myself, 'Thar's an axle-tree wants ilein', en I'll be blamed if it ain't over te Ebenezer Hicks's.' I went te the barn te see how the hoss war feelin', en I sez, 'Kin ye carry me over te Ebenezer Hicks's if I saddle ye?' But Henry Clay give a kick thet sot me wonderin' how I war ever goin' te git thar."

"Many people think the end of the world is at hand," said my mother.

"They do, fer a fact."

He paused a moment, then went on:

"But them thet's skeered air folks without faith. I ain't got no call fer te take loads from folks what's skeered. Summow I cain't carry 'em."

"The burdens of life are, indeed, hard to bear alone."

"They air so; en 'twixt you and me, marm, I'm jest a mite onsartin 'bout what it air 'flicts some folks. 'Pears like Satan skeers more folks 'n is ever won over by the Lord's goodness en mercy. Them thet's allers a-tremblin' ain't much account when it comes te strappin' the bellyband real hard; they don't never set tight in the saddle when they're called on te go plumb through a wilderness o' thistles."

After meditating again for a time, he resumed:

"But Ebenezer Hicks warn't a patchin' on Uriah Busby what lives yander at Black B'ar Creek. He war so skeered he sot to weepin' when he see me come in, en I never see a woman ez hoppin' mad ez Sereny Busby! I couldn't take no loads from Brother Busby; accordin' te my notion, he warn't settin' up under none, en jest ez soon ez I sot eyes on Sister Busby I see *she* hedn't hitched up to nothin' of any heft neither. She don't set still long enough. I 'low I war some dis'p'inted."

He laughed faintly; perhaps he wished to convey the impression that the burdens of life were not so dreadful, after all.

"I fear you had your trouble all for nothing," said my mother.

"Ye see, Brother Busby war skeered, en Sister Busby got her dander up. I never knowed a woman with red hair that war afeared o' man or beast."

"Mr. Busby must have been very much frightened," remarked my mother, smiling.

"Not so skeered but what he could talk. Si Jordan had his speech tuck plumb away, en I never see Sister Jordan so flustered. But she don't say much nohow. Sereny Busby she keeps the top a-spinnin' the livelong day. But I hev seen Uriah Busby caved in more'n oncet. I knowed 'em both afore they war married. If I wanted a woman sprightly with her tongue ez well ez with her hands, I'd take Sereny Busby fer fust ch'ice; if I wanted a woman what knows a heap en sez mos' nothin', I'd take Kezia Jordan. Human natur' ain't allers the same. I 'low Sister Busby's got the most eddication."

"But education never helps much if the heart is not in the right place."

"Thet thar's what I've allers said. 'Pears like sometimes Sereny Busby's heart's jest a leetle lopsided en wants re-settin', ez ye might say. But thar's a sight o' difference a-twixt one load en another. When I set with some folks what's in a heap o' trouble, I go away ez happy ez kin be, but when I hev te go away without ary a load, I feel mos' empty."

Here there was another spell of silence, but after a few sips from a third cup of coffee he continued:

" 'Pears like thar warn't never no heft te Sereny Busby's troubles. She don't give 'em no chance te set; en jest ez a duck's back goes agin water, her'n is set agin loads."

"The Lord has given her a cheerful mind; I think she has much to be thankful for."

"She hez, fer a fact. But I never kin tell jes' how her mind is a-workin'. She steps roun' ez spry ez kin be, hummin' fiddle tunes mos'ly; en when Brother Busby tuck te bed with thet fever what's mos' killed him, she kept on a-hummin', en some folks would a-said she war triflin', but she warn't. She give Uriah his med'cine mos' reg'lar, en mopped his head with cold water from the well, en made him appetizin' rabbit soup. The Bible sez the sperrit's willin' but the flesh is weak, but I don't see no failin' in a woman thet kin hum all day like a spinnin'-top. . . . But I allers kin tell what Kezia Jordan is a-thinkin', en thar ain't no two ways 'bout it; Sister Jordan kin sing hymns so ye want te give right up en die, ye feel so happy."

"She has something wonderful in her voice when she sings," said my mother; "I felt that when I heard her sing 'in meeting.' "

"I 'low Si Jordan ain't perttickler benev'lent, but Kezia Jordan counts fer more'n one in that 'ar house."

"I fear she has had a life of much care and trouble, and perhaps that is one reason why she is so good."

"Folks is born like we find 'em, marm. I've been nigh on thirty year wrastlin' with the sorrows o' life, en I ain't seen ary critter change his spots. A wolf don't look like a wild cat, en I never see a fox with a bob tail; en folks air like varmints: God Almighty hez marked 'em with His seal."

He looked round the room abstractedly, and then said:

"It's looks thet tells when a man's in trouble; en a heap o' tribulation keeps folks from hollerin'. Sister Jordan hez knowed trouble from away back. But thar's a tremenjous difference a-twixt her en Si Jordan. He kin talk en pray when he gits a-goin', en I've heared him when it looked like his flow o' words would swamp the hull endurin' meetin'; but when the risin' settled thar warn't much harm done no way. But jes' let Sister Jordan sing a hymn, en ye feel like the hull yearth war sot in tune."

"That is because she is so sincere," observed my mother gravely.

"Thet's a fact. I ain't never forgot the time when I hed thet spell o' sickness en felt ez if thar war nothin' wuth a-livin' fer. What with sickness, en the defeat o' Fremont, en them desperadoes cuttin' up over in Kansas, en the goin's on o' them Demicrats in Springfield, 'peared like I never would be good fer nothin' more. All te oncet the feelin' come over me te go over te Kezia Jordan's. Thet ud be 'bout ez much ez I could do, seein' I war like a chicken what's jes' pecked its way through the shell. I hedn't got ez fur ez the kitchen door when I heared her a-singin':

> " 'Come, thou Fount of every blessin',
>   Tune my heart te sing Thy praise.'

"Thet voice o' her'n set me a-cryin', en I sot right down on the door-steps, en thanked God fer all His goodness. Arter a while, she come out fer a bucket o' water.

" 'Good Land!' she sez; 'I'm right glad te see ye. Go right in; ye're jest in time fer dinner; I've got some real nice prairie-chicken en pum'kin pie; everything's mos' ready.'

"Soon as I went in she sez:

" 'Mercy on us, Elihu! I never see ye look so! Set right down, en tell me what ails ye; ye ain't been sick 'thout lettin' me know, hev ye?' "

"I like to have such a good Christian for my nearest neighbour," said my mother, with much feeling.

"I 'low she warn't allers a Christian. I war over at Carlinville when she heared Pete Cartwright fer the fust time, en the meetin'-house warn't big enough te hold the people. Sister Jordan warn't moved te sing any durin' the fust hymn, but she j'ined in the second, en arter thet Brother Cartwright tuck right holt, ez ye might say, en swung 'em till their feet tetched perdition.

" 'Yo're ripe,' he sez, holdin' out his fist, 'yo're ripe, like grain waitin' fer the reaper! Ye'll be mowed down, en the grain 'll be plumb divided from the chaff, en the Christians 'll be parted from the sinners.'

"The hull meetin' began to move like wheat a-wavin' in the wind. The preacher knowed Kezia Jordan fer a nat'ral-born Christian by her singin', fer he p'inted straight, en sez:

" 'Ye're at the cross-roads, sister; ye'll hev te choose one or t'other; en the years en the months air gone fer most o' ye, en thar's on'y this here hour left fer te choose. Which will it be? Will it be the road thet leads up yander, or the one thet leads down by the dark river whar the willers air weepin' night en day?'

"This war the turnin' p'int fer a good many; but the preacher warn't satisfied yet. He rolled up en went te work in dead arnest. He tole 'bout the fust coon hunt he ever see:

" 'Sinners,' he sez, 'is jes' like the coon asleep in thet tree—never dreamin' o' danger. But the varmint war waked all on a sudden by a thunderin' smell o' smoke, en hed te take te the branches. Someone climbs up the tree en shakes the branch whar the coon is holdin' on.' En right here Pete Cartwright slung his handkerchief over his left arm en sez, 'A leetle more, a leetle more, a l-e-e-e-tle more en the varmint's bound te drap squar' on te the dogs.' He shuck his arm three times—'down, down, down,' he sez, lettin' the handkerchief drap, 'down te whar the wailin' en gnashin' air a million times more terrible 'n the sufferin's o' thet coon.' "

The Load-Bearer bent forward and his face assumed a look of tragic intensity as he continued:

"A veil o' mournin' war a-bein' pulled down over the meetin'. He war takin' the people straight te jedgment, like a flock o' sheep, with the goats a-followin', usin' no dividin' line, for he put it to 'em:

" 'Whar would ye all be if this here floor war te slide right from under ye, leavin' ye settin' on the brink, with Time on one side en Etarnity on t'other?'

"The hull meetin' war shuck te pieces, some hollerin', some too 'flicted te set up; en I see nigh on twenty plumb fainted en gone."

Elihu Gest sighed as he sat back in his chair, and proceeded in his usual way:

"When the meetin' war over I sez te Sister Jordan, 'How air ye feelin' in sperrit?' En she sez, 'I've had more'n enough o' this world's goods!'

" 'I want te know!' sez I.

" 'Yes,' she sez, 'I don't never want no more.' En I see it war for everlastin'."

No one spoke for a long time.

At last he rose from his chair and moved towards the

door like one in a dream, his face wearing a look of almost superhuman detachment.

Then, just before passing out, he turned and said:

"I'll bid ye good-day, fer the present."

This visit made the day a memorable one for me, for I saw in Elihu Gest a human wonder; he opened up a world of things and influences about which I had never dreamed. And when he had disappeared down the road to the south, the way he had come, I wondered how he was carrying his loads, what they could be, and whether my mother felt relieved of any of her burdens. But I held my peace, while she simply remarked:

"A very strange but very good man. I wonder if we shall ever see him again?"

Here was a man who did everything by signs, tokens, impressions; who was moved by some power hidden from the understanding of everyone else—a power which none could define, concerning which people had long since ceased to question. He came and went, influenced by signs in harmony with his own feelings and moods, by natural laws shut off from our understanding by the imperative rules of conventional religion and society. Things which were sealed mysteries to us were finger-posts to him, pointing the way across the prairies, in this direction or in that. Is it time to go forth? He would look up at the heavens, sense the state of Nature by the touch of the breeze, sound the humour of the hour with a plumb-line of his own, then set out to follow where it led.

The Load-Bearer's presence, his odd appearance, his descriptions and peculiar phrases, his spells of silence, his sudden enthusiasms, the paradox of humour and religious feeling displayed, brought to our home the fervour and candour of the meeting-house—honest pioneer courage and frankness, and, above all, an influence that left on me an impression never to be effaced. How far, how very far, we were from the Episcopal rector, with his chosen words, studied phrases, and polite and dignified sympathy! How far it all was from anything my parents had ever dreamed of even in so remote a country! The prairie was inhabited by a people as new and strange as the country itself.

And what a gulf there was between the customs of the old country and the customs usual in the new West! Visitors appeared unannounced and at almost any hour. To-day a neighbour would come two miles to borrow some sugar; to-morrow another would come still farther to borrow tea or coffee. All were received as if they were old and tried friends. My mother attended to the wants of those who came to borrow things for the table, while my father did his best to satisfy the men who came to borrow ploughs, spades, saws, wagons, and even horses.

For the neighbours considered my father a rich man, judging him by the horses, sheep, and cattle he owned. And when he appeared at meetings, wearing a handsome velvet waistcoat with rich blue checks—one of the waistcoats he purchased during his visit to Paris before his marriage—they thought him richer still.

Thus are appearances even more deceptive and dangerous than words, for all, without exception, are judged by the illusions produced by property and personal attire.

Chapter III

The Log-House

THE Log-House was built some twenty-five years before we came to live in it, but we never knew who planted the trees and flowers. Surely it must have been a lover of Nature, for these we know by the little signs and tokens they leave behind them. Certain flowers were omitted, such as the rose, the flower of fashion and convention, the one with least suggestive influence on the heart and the affections, for it always turns the thoughts on more personal and worldly things.

There is a law of correspondence, a kind of secret code proper for each condition of life, and people become distorted and confused when this law is ignored. How often I wanted to know who planted these flowers! I thought I could guess how the woman looked—for it certainly was a woman—and I fancied I could see her arriving here from the South with her husband, the couple intent on leading a quiet life, the husband raising stock instead of wheat and corn, the wife attending to household duties and to the planting and watering of the flowers—the old familiar ones which harmonised with the prairie and the inmost instincts of the soul.

I seem to see a tall, spare woman, with a pensive face,

as silent and psychic as Kezia Jordan, planting the flowers
in the first warm spell of the first April, in the evenings,
after supper, when the earth that had waited her coming
for æons and æons yielded up the fragrance of that marvellous loam composed of withered grass and flowering
weeds. Her husband is seated in an old rocking-chair in
the kitchen getting all the music he can out of a raspy
fiddle, a bloodhound lying on the floor beside him. The
wife plants only those flowers that have wistful eyes and
homely souls, and with every one a thought goes out that
fills a void between the past and the present, as she says
to herself: "That is the way they were at home." For the
silent figure, intent on digging with her own hands the
holes for the seeds and young plants, is thinking of one
who planted flowers of the same kind years before, far
away in another part of the country. And so she works
through the warm evenings, placing each thing, not
according to any rule of art, but according to memory and
the promptings of instinct. For the yard around the Log-
House was not disfigured with walks made by measure
and strewn with sand and shells. Everything grew as if
by nature, and this freedom gave the place a character of
its own which the slightest show of conventional art would
have made impossible. The sweet-william grew in great
high bunches, interlaced with the branches of other
shrubs, and the jimpson-weed and sumac were not far off,
under which the chickens stood and cleaned their feathers,
and where, on rainy days, they lent an air of gloom to the
surroundings.

And now that the silent figure has planted the summer
flowers, she thinks of the last and most important of all,

the morning-glory. This she places at each side of the north door, where in the future it will be the only green thing on that side of the house, excepting one large locust tree. But the morning-glory! With what care she waters the plant when the ground is dry, and how she looks forward to the day when it will be full of bloom, covering each side of the door, reminding her of the old homestead and absent friends!

And thus the last planting is done, and she steps inside and sits down beside her husband, musing for awhile, as my own mother would now do before beginning some new work.

How does it happen that between people who are strangers to one another there should be a connecting link of sympathy, forged by little acts like the planting of a certain flower, at a special time, in a special place? Perhaps there is a secret and invisible agreement between certain persons and places, a definite meaning in the coming and going of certain persons we have never seen, and that nothing is wholly futile. However it may be, the flower that was planted on the north side of the house by someone years before seemed planted there as much for my special benefit as for anyone else's.

One day, after breakfast, my attention was arrested by a sight which gave me a thrill of admiration. The morning-glories were in bloom! There they were, like a living vision, revealing to me something in the kingdom of flowers I had never seen or felt before. The radiant days of summer had decked the Log-House with a mantle more beautiful than any worn by the Queen of Sheba or by Solomon when he received her. And now, as the days were growing more languid and the evenings more wistful, autumn, with her endless procession of far, faint shadows, would steal across the threshold under a canopy of infinite and indescribable colour.

How the spell of their magic changed the appearance of the house! The flowers looked out on sky and plain with meek, mauve-tinted eyes, after having absorbed all the amaranth of a cloudless night, the aureole of early morning, and a something, I know not what, that belongs to dreams and distance wafted on waves of colour from far-away places. At times the flowers imparted to the rugged logs the semblance of a funeral pyre, their beauty suggesting the mournful pomp of some martyr-queen, with pale, wondering eyes, awaiting the torch in a pallium of purple. They gave to the entrance a sort of halo that symbolised the eternal residuum of all things mortal and visible.

How impressive around the Log-House was that hour of the evening when, just after sundown, the birds, the chickens, and the turkeys began to seek a resting-place for the night! With the gradual dying away of sound and movement, everything was tinged with mourning. When at last, with the slowly fading twilight, the fluttering of wings and chirping ceased, a vague stillness evoked a feeling of mystery that spread over the house and everything around it.

Now and again the quiet was broken by the sharp whiz of insects darting here and there through the gloaming, the cry of the whip-poor-will, as it flitted between the house and the hollow, or the far, lonesome call of the hoot-owl, followed by a puff of wind, the rustling of grass, and a period of nameless unrest, during which the crickets and the katy-dids began their long, languid litanies of the night.

Then, on certain evenings, a faint glow in the east would appear, and above the horizon the dawn of moon-rise gradually illumined the borders of the wilderness. In a few moments more an immense crimson disc looked out on the silence from behind great sheets of blood-red clouds, presently merging into amber, with stripes of silver and gold. But these colours would soon give place to a serene glow, and from that time until daybreak all Nature was wrapped in phantasmal twilight, the Log-House looming like a spectral silhouette in the silver light, its rugged logs heaped together like something in a dream, on the borders of a world apart, haunted by gliding shadows and illusive sounds.

Inside the house, after supper, when everything was put in order for the night, the stillness was oppressive, for the quiet was not that of repose. It suggested an immense and immeasurable sadness, and my mother would sit knitting in silence, with thoughts of the far-absent ones. About ten o'clock my father would read the evening prayers from the Anglican prayer-book, with the whole family kneeling, and I wondered what efficacy written prayers could have. But whenever I heard my mother utter the words: "May the Lord in His goodness have mercy on us!" I felt an instant accession of power. The words, coming from that magical voice, unlocked the reservoirs of the infinite, and faith came rushing through the flood-gates. They brought a presence which filled the house with hope and comfort. I was satisfied without being able to explain why. There were moments when she

seemed to bring a superhuman power to the threshold of
the Log-House beyond which danger and despair could
not enter. She had implicit faith in what she called the
"Promises." "The Lord in His mercy will never permit
it," she used to say when a calamity seemed inevitable;
and with all her sorrows the irreparable never happened.
Faith and prayer form a bulwark around the lives of some
people through which no permanent misfortune ever
penetrates.

Sometimes, after the evening prayers, the house became
subdued to a stillness which produced the effect of someone having crept in by stealth. The flames had gone from
the logs; the embers were smouldering into ashes; the
light and sparkle had turned to something that resembled
audible thought. This was the hour when the things which
during the day gave forth no noticeable sound now
seemed to speak or to chant. The stroke of the old clock,
with its long pendulum, went like a plummet to the
depths of the soul. It brought forth that part of Nature
which is hidden from our sight by a thin veil behind
which we can sometimes hear the voices on the other side.
The cry of the cricket was that of a tiny friend, affecting
only the smallest nerves of silence, but the solemn tones
of the time-piece accentuated our isolation. Some clocks
are nervous and rasping, others emit a tone of hope and
serenity, but the one in the Log-House had a deep, portentous tone which filled one with a sense of the hollowness
of things, the futility of effort, a consciousness of days and
nights continually departing, of vanishing memories, and
of people passing into lonely, isolated, and everlasting

dreams. A great gulf now separated us from the rest of the world, and my mother sat like one under a spell.

About midnight the stillness became an obsession. All Nature was steeped in an atmosphere of palpable quiet, teeming with dismal uncertainty and sombre forebodings. The flickering of a tallow candle added something ghostly to the room with its dark mahogany furniture, while every unfamiliar sound outside startled the members of the family who were still awake. The doleful duets of the katy-dids often came to a sudden stop, and during the hush it seemed as if anything might happen—the apparition of a phantom, or the arrival of a band of masked marauders. An owl would visit the solitary locust tree which stood between the north door and the barn, and its weird calls sent a shiver through the night. The first note had an indescribable quality, and the series of half-veiled trumpet calls that followed produced on me a sensation never to be forgotten. They sounded like nothing else in Nature, and came to me as a lament from some waif of the wilderness.

"Hear me, hear me, inhabitants of the Log-House! Is solitude now your portion?"

Again, in the dead of night, some animal would carry off a fowl, and the long-drawn-out "caws" came like the cries of a child for help, growing less and less distinct, and at last dying away in the distance as the animal passed the barn and began the descent into the hollow towards the woods. The effect on me was one of nervous apprehension. It was the mystery which added a nameless dread to a mere incident of the night.

On stormy nights in the autumn the north wind brought with it voices that moaned and sighed. Every sweep of the wind came with a chorus of lamentations that moved round and round, first on one side then on the other, and the intervals of silence between the gusts came as respites before some final disaster. The big locust, that stood alone, had an ominous whistle, while the trees and bushes at the front and back swayed under the low, swooping gusts, until the Log-House seemed once more a part of the wild and primitive forest.

At times streaks of cold light from the semi-circling moon would fall through the window on the old rag-carpet—old, because each strip had belonged to garments worn long before the carpet was put together. It needed the moonlight or the soft rays of the setting sun to bring out all its romance and mystery. Then the stripes of saffron evoked the presence of Kezia Jordan, and the darker hues memories of the Load-Bearer, Socrates, and Minerva Wagner. What romantic adventure these patches suggested! I would sit and count the pieces and compare one colour with another, for each seemed imbued with a personality of its own. Here, in the common sitting-room, filled with chimeras about to vanish, each strip of cloth was as a pillow for some dead thing of the past, some greeting or regret. There were strips worn when the wearer set sail from the old country, others had faced a hail of bullets at Buena Vista, passed through an Indian rising, or the first stormy meetings of the Abolitionists in Illinois. Once all these strips of cloth had stood for life and action; they wrapped a world of dreams and moods, but now they covered a rough floor in a house of logs.

They humanised the interior as graves humanise a plot of earth. And never did sacred carpet of Mecca contain so much of the magic of life; for here, too, daily prayers were said on bended knee, and the carpet seemed one with the religious aspirations of the occupants, with all our hopes and fears, joys and sorrows.

How genial and home-like it was! It belonged to the order of the wild roses and flowering weeds, the corn and clover, the morning-glories, the jimpson, the sumac, and the red-winged blackbirds that soared in circles around and above the house.

If its shreds and patches suggested things of the past, the Log-House life it represented was palpitating with the present: full of human dreams and ambitions, of the voiceless sentiments that make a home in the bosom of the prairie. It invited the tired wayfarer of the lonely roads to come in and be refreshed with steaming coffee and hot biscuits, pound-cake, and dainty pies made from the products of the loamy soil; it invited all to step in and listen to words of encouragement if in trouble, and words of sympathy if in affliction; for the rag-carpet was made for the Log-House, and the Log-House was made for Man.

Chapter IV

Socrates Gives Advice

THE day Socrates made his first call at the Log-House I happened to be at home, instead of fishing a mile away, or wandering about in my accustomed haunts among the squirrels, birds, and rabbits. He brought Ebenezer Hicks with him.

Socrates entertained me with some simple stories of his experience as a hunter and trapper twenty or thirty years earlier: how he killed big game during the winters of the great snows, his buffalo hunts in Missouri and Iowa, his strange devices for snaring the mink, the fox, and the raccoon.

I devoured every word with eager excitement: here was the actual romance of the wild woods.

"And have you killed many bitterns and owls?" I inquired.

"I don't b'lieve in killin' things ye cain't eat or skin."

It seemed to me that this Socrates of the wilderness had something of the look of a big horned owl, with his bushy eyebrows and short scraggy beard. Over his sparsely covered head the years had cast a halo of experience and wisdom, and I began to respect this man who united in himself so much adventure and common sense. He seemed strong as a lion and harmless as a lamb, free as the winds of the prairie, yet methodical and never in doubt. He brought with him into the Log-House—where our family had gathered like a flock of sheep in a strange land —a feeling of security and a renewal of faith and courage.

"There's not much need of raising stock in this part of the country," said my father jokingly; "game is so plentiful."

"The new settlers air givin' tharselves a heap o' trouble jes' fer the fun o' ploughin' en reapin'. They snap the bow-strings. They air tryin' te kill big game with a shot-gun, en the shot scatters all over the kintry. It air good 'nough fer rabbits en squirrels, but it don't stop a buck jumpin' er a b'ar from browsin'. I see a heap o' hard work fer some o' these here settlers what's comin' in from the ole kintries over East. 'Tain't wisdom.

"Some folks air too good fer this world 'thout bein' plumb ready fer the nex'. Accordin' te thar reasonin', a prairie-chicken settin' on the fence air better'n two birds o' paradise over yander. The world air a sorrowin' vale, kase folks hez too many stakes in the groun'. Ez fer me, I kin shoot en trap all I kin eat, jes' plantin' 'nough corn fer hoe-cakes en a leetle fodder, en some taters en turnips en pum'kins; en I hev a sight more smoked venison en b'ar meat in winter than I kin eat ez a single man with on'y one stommick; en I 'low I kin give a traveller hoe-cakes en fried chicken all he wants to fill up on."

Socrates sat like a lump of hewn adamant, his look alone being sufficient guarantee of his ability to take care of himself without the slightest trouble or worry.

"Thar be folks that air trampin' over these prairies

a-spadin' up trouble like thar warn't none te be hed by
settin' down in the city en lettin' other folks bring it to
'em. Thar's a heap too much corn en wheat, a durned
sight too many kyows en hosses; en the four-legged
critters chaws up what the two-legged critters gathers in.
It air wus nor dog eat dog, seein' ez how the four-legged
critters air livin' on the fat o' the land while the pore
planters air livin' on spar' ribs en hens with sinoos ez
tough ez b'iled owels."

"But it makes a great difference when a man has a
family to support and educate," remarked my mother,
thinking of the responsibility of parents.

"I allow readin' en writin' air a good thing if ye've got
any figurin' to do; but cipherin's a drefful load on the
mind. Thar's Si Jordan yander; he sets figurin' o' nights,
en calculatin' te see jes' how he'll come out at the end o'
the year; but I allers say to myself he's like the groun'-
hog, he won't come out."

"Still, it would be awkward to have to calculate with
nothing but your fingers," observed my father, smiling.

"Fingers or no fingers, book-larnin' don't make a man
no better than he war in a state o' natur'. Them as reads
newspapers knows too much 'bout other folks's sins en
not 'nough 'bout thar own. Over Decatur en Fancy Creek
way they built meetin'-houses with steeples on 'em, en the
wimin-folks tuck te wearin' store clothes en the men-folks
put on b'iled shirts. But when the comet come into view
the wimin put on their ole sun-bonnets, allowin' pink
calico te be more'n enough te be jedged in."

My mother, as she looked up from her knitting,
thought his round grey eyes seemed bigger and rounder

than ever. She noticed in his face an expression of naïve irony and unconscious satire which she had not remarked before. But later there radiated from his face a sense of pity when he thought of all the hard work she would have to do. In some unaccountable way he had come into touch with the unexpressed hopes and fears of the silent man sitting before him, and the pale, passive face of his wife, who was knitting.

Then, as if struck with a sudden, new idea, he said:

"Ye kin divide the day's doin's into two passels—the happenin's en the fac's; en thar ain't but two leadin' fac's in all creation—bein' born en bein' dead. Howsomever, right in betwixt 'em thar's some purty lively happenin's a-steppin' roun' on all fours, ez when a panther takes a notion te drap on a pig's back; it's a shore thing fer the panther but a dead loss fer the owner. En it air jest ez sartin the fact air plumb again the pig, but he don't live long 'nough te know it. Thar's been a suddin burial, en the mourner kin see the fact, but he ain't never see the corpse. Anyhow, it's an argiment thet'll work itself out ez easy ez a groun'-worm arter rain, en it don't make no pertickler difference which end comes up fust, heads en tails bein' purty nigh ekil."

My father enjoyed a hearty laugh, and my mother stopped knitting and eyed Socrates as if trying to fathom the secret of his strange originality.

"It beats my time all holler," he went on, "te see folks so kind o' waverin' en onsartin. Instead o' waitin' fer the last hour they make fer it with thar heads down like a bull agin a red flag, en no tail-twistin' 'll stop 'em. Thar's skasely a settler among the new uns but what'll tell ye

they air workin' te live. It air workin' te die, thet's what
I call it."

"Thar's a good many workin' land they ain't got no
title to," remarked Ebenezer Hicks.

"When I go te meetin'," said Socrates, "en hear some
o' these settlers sing about readin' thar title cl'ar te mansions in the skies I allers feel like askin' 'em how they're
holdin' on te the land they got; kase thar ain't but two
kyinds o' settlers—them ez buys right out, and them ez
squats right down, en I've allers found thet hymn air a
dead favourite among the people thet set right down jes'
whar thar feet begin te swell.

"What I know 'bout Bible-teachin' air plumb agin
squatters takin' up land t'other side Jordan. The Lord
God hez issued a writ statin' His objections. I ain't never
knowed a real live Yankee thet war any good at squattin'.
They come from below the Ohio, whar they hev seen the
niggers do all the work. En when they come up to this
kintry they sing about readin' thar title cl'ar te big slices
o' land in the nex' world! I tell ye what it is, if thar's ever
goin' te be war it'll be betwix' them thet wants the land
fer nothin' en them thet wants it fer sunthin', if it ain't
fer more'n shootin' snipe en plover. The squatters air
lazy; en t'other folks, like the Squar hyar, air killin'
tharselves by doin' too much.

"My ole daddy larnt me te go through this sorrowin'
vale like the varmints do—easy en nat'ral like, never gal-
lopin' when ye kin lope, en never lopin' when ye kin lay
down. It's a heap easier. Thar ain't a hog but knows he
kin root fer a livin' if ye give him a fair show; thar ain't a
squirrel but knows how te stow away 'nough te nibble on

when he wakes up en finds his blood's kinder coolin' down en things is p'intin' te zero."

After a pause he looked hard at my father, and put the question abruptly:

"What'll ye do, Squar, when ye plough up the prairie thar nex' year, en sow it with corn ez ye calc'late on doin'? How d'ye 'low ye'll git all the work done 'thout extry hands?"

It was an unexpected query that left my father without an immediate answer. He had never given the subject any serious thought.

Socrates continued without waiting for explanations:

"Ye'll hev a heap o' corn-huskin' te do, en ye suttingly ain't a-goin' te reckon on thet leetle lady with them hands o' her'n doin' much corn-huskin' en sech. 'Pears like she'll hev more'n enough te keep her a-goin' right in the house."

My mother was thinking: "The Lord's will be done. He had a reason for sending us here; some day we may know *why*."

Socrates resumed:

"Hirin' extry hands means payin' out a lot o' money; mebbe yer purse-strings air like yer latch-string, en mebbe ye got a plenty te last ye till nex' harvest time. Things ain't like they war; folks useter come twenty mile to a corn-huskin', en the doin's ud end up with eatin' en drinkin' en dancin'. Now people air too busy with thar own funerals. They useter help other people work thar-selves to death; now they stay at home en dig thar own graves 'thout borrowing shovels er sendin' fer a fiddler te help 'em mourn with thar tired feet. I keep sayin' the comet may pass over 'thout drappin'; but if the politicioners, en the lawyers, en them ez sez they don't know nothin', en the hordes o' settlers thet cain't tell the difference betwix' a yaller dog en a long-eared rabbit ain't a-bringin' the world to a spot stop, then Zack Caverly hez missed fire, en it'll be the fust time."

"As for that," said my father, "it certainly does look as if some great change would soon come over the country. Many are turning to religion for consolation, while others predict civil war."

"I see some cussed mean folks pretendin' te hev religion. Some on 'em air thet deceivin' I allers feel like watchin' em with a spy-glass till they git into the woods en then sendin' my old hound arter 'em te see they don't commit bigamy er hang themselves right on my diggin's."

"Wal," said Ebenezer Hicks, who had been listening attentively, "I 'low ye've tetched a festern sore when ye say some on 'em air ekil te committin' treason en blasphemy, but ez fer me I hev allers been a church member; but some folks ain't never satisfied te leave things ez they wur. It's my opinion all the trouble hez come about in the Church by them busybodies mixin' up religion with politics. Abolition hez been a bone o' contention en a skewer through both wings o' the Methodists. You war thar when Azariah James preached thet sermon, windin' up by h'istin' the Abolition flag, en you too, Squar, en you heared what he said."

"Ye'll allow he hed all creation te h'ist on," remarked Socrates; "the stars en stripes te begin with, two kyinds o' lawyers en four kyinds o' preachers—all on 'em off'n whisky. T'other party ain't got no flag, but thar whisky makes 'em see the stars en they make the niggers feel the stripes."

Ebenezer Hicks, wishing to turn the conversation, simply observed:

"Over at Bloomington en Springfield the people air all fer Lincoln."

But Socrates held to the subject and went on:

"What beats my time is te know what you folks hez te do with the nigger question anyway. Did ye ever own any slaves?"

"Nary a one."

"Wal, then, what difference does it make te you whether they work ez slaves er work ez we uns work? Looks like ye belong te them thet's pinin' away kase ye ain't got sorrers enough o' yer own te hitch to. When we all heared Azariah James preach—the on'y time the meetin'-house hez been open all summer—I see right away we'd got plumb into the middle o' the Abolition circus en someone ud turn a somerset afore he got through. Fact is, the people o' this here State air a-gettin' ready te send Abe Lincoln te Washington, en ole Buchanan's jes' keepin' the presidential cheer from warpin' till Abe comes."

"That preacher, Azariah James," said my father, "was not such a fool as some of the congregation thought he was."

"Not nigh," returned Socrates, as he rose from his seat and took his leave.

A few days after his visit my mother remarked:

"Now, I suppose, we shall not have any more visitors

for a long time. There are days when I wish someone would call, and somehow I have been thinking a good deal of Mrs. Jordan lately. I should like a visit from her more than from anyone else I know just at present."

That same afternoon, as I was returning to the house from the hollow where I had been gathering hazel-nuts, I thought I could discern a stranger through the window. I entered the house and found Kezia Jordan seated in the rocking-chair.

Once more her presence opened the door to a world that transcended all the familiar forms of speech; for it was not what she said but what she looked that impressed me so profoundly.

Moulded and subdued by the lonely days, the monotonous weeks, the haunting hush of the silent nights, and the same thoughts and images returning again and again, she appeared as one who had conquered the world of silence. Elihu Gest partly explained himself by his explanation of others, but Kezia Jordan made few comments, and they were rarely personal. She never talked for the sake of talking. As she sat there she might have been a statue, for to-day she brought with her an inexorable detachment from worldly thoughts and influences.

The sentiments she inspired in me were like those produced by the motion of clouds on a calm, moonlight night, or the falling of leaves on a still, dreamy day of Indian summer. There were moments when her presence seemed to possess something preternatural, when she imparted to others an extraordinary and superhuman quietude. Her spirit, freed for ever from the trammels and tumults of the world, seemed heedless of the passing moments, resigned to every secret and mandate of destiny; for hers was a freedom which was not attained in a single battle—the conflict was begun by her ancestors when they landed at Plymouth Rock. In the tribulations that followed the successive generations were stripped of the superfluities of life. One by one vanities and illusions fell from the fighters like shattered muskets and tattered garments. Each generation, stripped of the tinsel, became acquainted with the folly of plaints and the futility of protests. Little by little the pioneers began to understand, and in the last generation of all there resulted a knowledge too deep for discussion and a wisdom too great for idle misgivings.

Where was the hurried visitor from foreign lands who could sound the depths of such a soul?

The influences were different when Mrs. Busby came to the Log-House. She brought with her pleasant maxims about her bakings, her messes, and herb-medicines, and talked on and on without caring what the subject was. She created commotion and movement, and under her hands the kettle hissed and spouted.

Mrs. Jordan handled things as if they had life and feeling, and without being conscious of influencing others she brought with her a power that penetrated to the core of things. She had passed the time when her duties had to be accomplished by the aid of a strenuous use of the reasoning faculties. She had arrived at that stage when religion was not a thing of reason, but a state of perpetual feeling. Circumstances altered, conditions changed and found her the same, unaltered and unalterable.

Yet she had her day-dreams, moments of rapt meditation which bordered on forgetfulness, when the formless visions and homely realities of kitchen, meeting-house, and prairie became one, and the song of the blackbird and the chirping of the cricket seemed a part of her own life and feeling. She possessed the dominant influence of an abiding power with a total absence of self-assertion, for hers was that true power of the soul, an influence that penetrates to depths which intellect alone can never reach.

I thought the rocking-chair was made for Kezia Jordan, and the rag-carpet too, and somehow I could never quite free my mind from the impression that the flowers about the house were hers as well.

Soon after my arrival a rap was heard at the door, and in walked Minerva Wagner, proud, lean, wrinkled, and unbending. She came within the category of those who, according to Zack Caverly, were labouring under the necessity of borrowing trouble. She had not yet recovered from the shock produced by the Abolition sermon of the preacher, Azariah James. Mrs. Wagner was our nearest neighbour to the north, and every time I glanced in that direction I would marvel at the listless, lonely life of the family in the little frame house stuck like a white speck on the brow of the prairie, ten times more lonely and isolated than the Log-House we inhabited. Whenever I saw some-one moving about over there I thought of a tomb opening its doors and letting out an imprisoned ghost; for every member of the family looked and walked and talked alike, except, perhaps, old Minerva Wagner, who stood to-day facing the inexorable present—stern, relentless, unable to account for anything she saw or heard, but choking with prejudice against what she persisted in calling "the Yankee trash of Indianny and Illinoise."

After some talk about pickles and bacon and apple-butter, and some allusion to the awful state of the country, brought on by the Anti-Slavery agitation, Mrs. Wagner took her departure, and once more the room assumed the calm, peaceful aspect commensurate with Kezia Jordan's presence. My mother made tea, and the moments passed as if there were no clock ticking the time away and no regrets for the old days that would never return; and when at last Mrs. Jordan rose from her seat she looked more slender than ever in her simple dress of copperas-coloured jean; and when the clouds parted and the setting sun shone full on the windows, her spare figure cast a shadow that fell across the rag-carpet, and there, under her feet, were strips of coloured cloth, the counterpart of her own dress, and it seemed as if she had always belonged to the Log-House and ought never to leave it.

Chapter V

Silas Jordan's Illness

THE solemn hush of the wilderness had its voices of bird and insect, wind, rain, and rustling grass; but from the song of birds and grasshoppers to the noiseless march of the comet was a far and terrible cry, and more than one head of a family, seeing it approach nearer and nearer to the earth, sat with folded hands awaiting the end. While it frightened some into silence it made others loquacious, while others again could not help laughing at the comical figure some of the frightened ones assumed.

No sooner did Silas Jordan see the comet than a great fear seized him, and he sat down in the kitchen, a millstone of desolation holding him in his seat.

Hardly a day passed that I did not run up to the Jordans', and on this evening, instead of hearing Mrs. Jordan singing one of her favourite hymns, I listened to a monologue which contained a note of sadness.

When Kezia came in with a chicken which she had just killed and was about to scald and pluck, a glance at her husband told her of the great and sudden change.

"Dear me suss! Zack Caverly said ye'd be apt to feel a touch o' fever when ye broke that piece o' land down by the Log-House."

She expected an answer, but none came, and she went on:

"I don't know what we'll do with so much work waitin' to be done."

She took from the highest shelf in the cupboard a large box of quinine pills and offered Silas two, but he refused them with a stubborn shake of the head.

Mrs. Jordan put the box aside and began to pluck the chicken with a will that might have inspired her husband with courage had he noticed what she was doing.

"It ain't no use givin' way and broodin' over yer feelin's," she said quietly.

Alek came in and told his mother a comet was to be seen, and she stepped to the door to look.

She had heard the rumours and prophecies, but they left her indifferent. Her deep religious faith made it impossible for her to worry when worry seemed almost a sin, and it never occurred to her that Silas was not ill of malaria, but of fear and despair.

"Pap's ailin'," said Alek. "If he ain't no better tomorrer I'll go fer that yarb doctor that cured Ebenezer Hicks o' them faintin' spells."

He had a horror of long illnesses, and would call in a "doctor" at the slightest sign of a break-up in health.

The next day I was at the Jordan home again, this time with tempting eatables for the invalid, who, however, refused everything.

The doctor arrived shortly after; then, on his heels, came Socrates, who, when he saw the doctor's horse and saddle-bags, guessed there was something wrong with the Jordan household.

The doctor was looking about the room like a rabbit let

loose in a strange place. Lank and bony, clothed in blue jeans, he looked a picture of unsophisticated ignorance.

"My husband's ailin'," said Mrs. Jordan, as she took a chair and placed it before Silas for the doctor.

"How long's he been feelin' this a-way?" he asked in a drawling voice as he sat down and took hold of the patient's limp hand.

"Sence yesterday."

"Chills en fever, I reckon," he said, looking at Silas with a blank stare.

"He ain't had any chills," returned Mrs. Jordan.

"Ain't hed no pin-feather feelin's?"

"I don't reckon he hez."

"No chatterin' o' the teeth?"

"Not ez I know of."

"Been wanderin' in his mind?"

"Not ez I know of."

"Ain't felt overly het up?"

"I guess not."

"Then I reckon it's dumb ague," concluded the doctor, at his wits' end.

"I guess it is," said Kezia, "fer he ain't spoke a word sence he was took."

The doctor now asked to see the patient's tongue, and after much persuasion Silas slowly put out the tip, then closed his jaws with a smart snap.

"Mighty peert fer a man thet cain't talk," observed Zack Caverly. But the doctor, more and more bewildered, simply nodded his head, and then moved his chair back several paces as if to be well out of the reach of a patient who might suddenly do him an injury.

He looked fixedly at the little wiry-faced man, not knowing what to say or do.

Suddenly a thought struck him.

"Hez he ever hed quare idees?"

"I don't know thet he hez, 'ceptin' he's been figurin' on jest how long it would take to buy out the folks at the big Log-House."

"En ye say he ain't et no vittles sense yestiddy?"

"Not a morsel."

The doctor considered for a while, pulled at his goatee, and said:

"I 'low his symptomania air summat confoundin', but jest at this pertickler p'int whar, ez ye might say, the fever hez kinder thawed out the chills, en the chills hez sorter nipped the fever in the bud, both on 'em hev been driv' in. They're a-fightin' it out on the liver, en a man ain't calc'lated te know jest how things air a-workin' up on the inside."

"Will it last long?" demanded Alek.

"Wal, thar ain't no cause to be frustrated. T'other day I see a man over B'ar Creek way thet rolled on the floor fer nigh an hour, en I'm doggoned if the chills en fever didn't stay right whar they war. His wife allowed I hed giv' him too much senna en calomel, but it takes a powerful sight te make 'em go different ways—more pertickler when the chills air dumb."

The doctor, after ordering huge doses of calomel and quinine, shuffled awkwardly out, and Socrates took Silas Jordan's hand and considered for a moment. Then, looking about the room, he observed:

"If chills means bein' cold, he ain't got no chills, en if fever means bein' hot, he ain't got no fever."

"What hez he, then?" inquired Alek, with a startled look.

"He's got the funks!"

"I want to know!" exclaimed Kezia, rising to face the new situation.

Alek, appalled at the sound of a word he had never heard till now, gasped out:

"Is it ketchin'?"

"Ketchin'! I'd like te see ye ketch a weazil in a haystack," observed Zack Caverly.

Mrs. Jordan looked at one and then at the other, but before she had time to say anything further, in came Uriah Busby.

He had come in a great hurry.

Of middle age, somewhat portly, and slightly bald, he now looked ten years older than when I saw him at the meeting-house. To-day his face wore a haggard and woebegone expression.

Uriah Busby had come to find out what his practical, cool-headed neighbour, Silas Jordan, thought of the comet.

"Glad to see ye," was Kezia's gentle greeting.

She handed him a chair, and Uriah sat down, heaved a deep sigh, and began to wipe his perspiring head and face with his big handkerchief.

"No," resumed Socrates, where he had left off; "he ain't sick, he's only skeered."

Uriah Busby could hardly believe his ears. He had come, thinking that Silas Jordan would have some counsel of hope to offer, and there he sat scared into helplessness!

Nevertheless, Uriah felt called upon to say something:

"These be times of great affliction. It looks like the preacher war plumb right, en the Lord's hand is stretched agin us."

"Mebbe ye're right," interrupted Socrates; "but ez fur ez I kin see the Lord ain't tetched any of ye with more'n a thumb en forefinger."

The eyes of the invalid were now wide open; he sat bolt upright as if shaking off the effects of a horrid nightmare, and blurted out:

"Arter all, like ez not it ain't a-comin' our way!"

Uriah Busby pointed upward, his voice tremulous with emotion:

"Mebbe it's only a sign o' grace fer the elect."

But Socrates simply remarked: "It's a sign ye've been settin' on a chinee egg like a wet hen, en it's 'bout time ye war up en dustin'."

Kezia's dark face was all aglow; she looked as if she had no words to express what she felt.

Uriah Busby's confusion increased with every remark that came from Socrates, who seemed to expose everyone's secret.

"It's jest ez ye say," he stammered at last; "if the Lord's willin' it's our dooty te work en not te set waitin'."

"En he's been settin' there ever sence he was took," said Mrs. Jordan.

" 'Pears like ye'll hev te pull him up like ye would a jimpson-weed," added Socrates. "Mebbe thet med'cine man hez got more sense than I 'lowed he had; mebbe ez like ez not Si needs a thunderin' big shakin', en if we'll jes' set te work we kin bring him te rights. Did ye ever see a b'ar come out arter the fust big thaw, hoppin' roun' on two legs, this a-way, gettin' his sinoos sorter stretched en his blood sorter warmed up?"

He began to imitate a dancing bear, stepping first on one leg, then on the other, swaying, nodding, and bending his head, with comical glances at Silas.

"Do like mister b'ar; shake yerself!"

And with this he pulled the invalid out of his seat with a sudden jerk, forcing him round and round, dancing, bending, and hopping, with growls and grimaces to harmonise with his bruin-like antics.

"Keep it up," shouted Uriah Busby; "it'll do him a heap o' good."

Socrates kept up the hopping and swaying until Silas Jordan was exhausted and Alek's fear had changed into a broad grin that was almost laughter; and hardly had the mad dance ceased when Silas asked for fried chicken, the chicken which Kezia had killed and dressed, and kept for some such occasion.

"The ways o' the Lord air past findin' out," remarked Uriah, wiping his face.

When the chicken was ready Silas walked about picking a wing which he held in both hands.

"He's ez hungry ez a wolf, I do declare," said Kezia in a half-whisper, as she went about her duties, relieved of the long strain of watching and waiting. Then she added:

"I never see his ekil!"

"I 'low ye never did, Sister Jordan," rejoined Socrates; "but ye're mistaken in the varmint—ye mean he's ez hungry ez a catamount!"

Chapter VI

The Cabin of Socrates

"SONNY," said my father one afternoon, "you can come with me and you will have a chance of seeing Socrates, for I am to call at his cabin to see a drover on some business."

I accepted the invitation with joy, for I never tired of hearing Zack Caverly talk; even to sit and look at him was to me a great treat.

Socrates was sitting at his cabin door, smoking, dreaming, and listening to what strange sounds might reach him from the woods. As he sat there he felt himself detached from the world, yet near enough to human beings to have all the society he desired. He thought of the new settlers, their troubles and vexations, and he wondered how many of them were as free from care as himself.

Under the cabin the hounds were sleeping, all cuddled up, and now, after a somewhat busy and exciting day, Nature seemed more intimate and satisfying than ever. Age brought with it less and less ambition, less and less desire to do useless things, to speculate about vain theories and impending political events. To the mind of Socrates worry and ambition were unnatural and foolish things, and eternity meant to-day.

As he sat at his door he felt at home in the universe. The wilderness was his kingdom; his subjects, the birds and beasts; his friends, the hounds and his rifle; and he rode out among the settlers like a king on a tour of inspection, with advice here and a greeting of encouragement where it was needed, and when he returned to his cabin, peace and contentment issued forth from every log.

His cabin was his palace. A huge stag's head nailed over the entrance might have been taken for a coat-of-arms in the rough, while inside another set of antlers adorned the chimney-place. From the rafters hung the pelt of fox and wild cat; a low couch was covered with a buffalo robe, and on the floor were some old skins of the black bear. Several trophies of the wolf were stretched on nails, and strings of Indian corn hanging about here and there made the inside of the cabin a picture of indolence as well as activity.

Zack Caverly was the last of his peculiar mode of life in this part of the country, and towns and railroads would soon put an end to such a mode of living.

The cabin adjoined a deep wood not far from a creek, with the prairie in front, and from his door not a house could be seen.

Socrates had been here some twenty-five years, and knew the history of every family within a radius of many miles: their peculiarities, virtues, and vices. He could sum up the powers and failings of a newcomer at a glance. As for himself, he knew where his food would come from for a year, good weather or bad; he knew the work required at his hands, using his own time and pleasure in doing it. For often when the weather was fine, and the ground dry, he would spend whole days hunting in the bottoms, many miles from home. He ploughed when it suited him, and reaped much in the same way. He read no books, did not belong to any religious sect, never had been to school, and, owing to his wanderings in his younger days, had no prejudices.

He knew the haunts and habits of all the animals and birds of field and forest, and the time to expect certain wild flowers; and he had his own weather signs. He loved everything wild, regarding his solitary mode of life as the most natural thing in the world.

As the days and hours came and went, so he passed from one mood to another without being conscious of any change, without grief or regret, rising in the morning and lying down at night with the same feeling of security and contentment. And principally for this reason he was welcomed everywhere, bringing with him an atmosphere of mental vigour and confidence at a time when these forces were so much needed. His mind was on the present; thus no time was lost in idle sorrow for events of yesterday.

It was nearly dusk when we arrived at the cabin, and my father had not long to wait for the drover. Soon after Socrates set about getting us supper of bacon, eggs, hoe-cakes, and coffee, which we ate with keen appetites.

Shortly after supper was over Elihu Gest, the Load-Bearer, came driving up, and hitched his team to one of the logs near the door. He was on his way home from the post-office.

"I war kinder moved te come aroun' en see ye," he said.

"Right glad ye come; ye're allers welcome ez long ez

I'm alive en kickin'," answered Socrates, with his usual good humour.

"The feelin' come jest ez I got te the cross-roads, thar by Ebenezer Hicks's cornfield."

Just then Lem Stephens rode up.

Socrates had come out to greet the Load-Bearer, and the three men sat down on the logs while I sat at one side. My father and the drover were inside discussing some matters of business.

But oh! how shall I depict the company outside? the objects fading in the deepening dusk, the stars growing brighter every moment, the stillness broken now and again by the cries of the whip-poor-will and the conversation of the three men!

After a long spell of cloudy weather the sky had cleared; the air was warm and dry, and when darkness closed in the night came with a revelation. Never in that region had such a night been seen by living man, for a comet hung suspended in the shimmering vault, like an immense silver arrow, dominating the world and all the constellations.

An unparalleled radiance illumined the prairie in front of the cabin; the atmosphere vibrated with a strange, mysterious glow; and as the eye looked upward it seemed as if the earth was moving slowly towards the stars.

The sky resembled a phantasmagoria seen from the summit of some far and fabulous Eden. The Milky Way spread across the zenith like a confluence of celestial altars flecked with myriads of gleaming tapers, and countless orbs rose out of the luminous veil like fleecy spires tipped with the blaze of opal and sapphire.

The great stellar clusters appeared like beacons on the shores of infinite worlds, and night was the window from which the soul looked out on eternity.

The august splendour of the heavens, the atmosphere, palpitating with the presence of the All-ruling Spirit, diffused a feeling of an inscrutable power reaching out from the starry depths, enveloping the whole world in mystery.

I sat and gazed in awe and silence.

Socrates was quietly smoking a corn-cob pipe, while Elihu Gest, rapt in wonder, contemplated the heavens as if seeking an answer to his innermost thoughts.

"I knowed we war close to it," he exclaimed at last, referring to the comet; "the hand o' the Lord air p'intin' straight!"

He stopped to meditate again, and no one broke the silence for some little time.

Then he proceeded:

"I've seen it afore, but never like this. 'Pears like over around here the hull heavings air cla'rer, and the stars look like they war nigher the yearth."

"Be you on risin' groun'?" asked Lem Stephens, addressing Socrates.

"Not onless it's riz sence we've been settin' here."

"I allowed ye warn't," said Lem; "but I thought mebbe I war mistaken."

"It's the feelin's a man hez when mericles air a-bein' worked," said the Load-Bearer, with familiar confidence. "A man's thoughts en feelin's ain't noways the same when the Lord begins te manifest His power. He ain't afeared te show His hand; but I ain't never see a kyard-player thet'll let ye look at his kyards."

" 'Kase it air we uns thet do the shufflin'," observed Socrates; "Providence allers leads and allers wins. But some o' these settlers knows what spades air, I reckon."

"En some 'll suttingly know what clubs air if they keep on with thar nigger stealin'," spoke up Lem Stephens.

To this the Load-Bearer paid no attention. His thoughts were on the signs of the times and the man who was to lead in the great struggle.

"Thar's a new dispensation a-comin'," he said with calm conviction; "but it warn't made plain what it ud be till I heared Abe Lincoln en Steve Douglas discussin' some p'ints o' law fer the fust time. When I heared Lincoln war a-goin' te speak I sez: 'Now's yer time. If ye miss this chance ye won't mebbe hev another.' When I got thar I see Jedge Douglas war 'p'inted te open the meetin'."

"Thet give ye a chance te see how the Leetle Giant ud look alongside o' the six-footer," interrupted Socrates. "When I heared the Jedge he give chapter en verse for every hole he bored in the Republican plank; but when Abe Lincoln riz up he held some thunderin' big Abolition nails te plug 'em with. 'Peared like he ez much ez sez te Steve Douglas: 'You jes' keep on borin' en I'll do the drivin'; it's a heap easier; fer when you fellers git through borin' I'll hev my plank nailed te the constitution o' this hull kintry!' "

"I 'low Steve Douglas hed the law on his side," rejoined Elihu Gest; "but lawyer Lincoln hedn't been speakin' more'n ten minutes afore I see he war a-bein' called on, en 'peared like I could hear the words, 'jedgment, jedgment!' a-soundin' in the air; en if all the prairies o' this here State hed been sot on fire, I'd a-sot thar till he'd a-spoke the last word!"

"Shucks!" exclaimed Socrates; "I don't reckon Steve Douglas keers; but I 'spect he see it warn't no use sassin' back."

Lem Stephens struck the log several hard, quick blows with his wooden leg.

"But laws! What kin words en book-larnin' do agin the Ten Commandments?" ejaculated the Load-Bearer.

"I reckon Jedge Douglas war relyin' on saft sodder; but it won't hold the spout te the kittle if the fire's anyways over het and the water's mos' b'iled away," said Socrates.

"Ez I war a-goin' te say," continued Elihu Gest, " 'tain't words ez counts ez much ez it air the feelin's. A politician's 'bout the same in this here ez a preacher: he hez te possess the sperrit if he wants the power. Accordin' te my thinkin' he hez te throw it out till it kivers the hull meetin'."

"I b'lieve ye're right," assented Socrates nonchalantly. "I've heared the Leetle Giant more'n oncet, en I 'low he did look spry en plump, en ez boundin' ez a rubber ball. But it ain't the hoss thet jumps the highest thet kin carry the furdest, en I reckon a man's got te be convicted hisself afore he convicts ary other."

"The sperrit air more in th' eye than it air in the tongue," said Elihu Gest, rising from his seat; "if Abe Lincoln looked at the wust slave-driver long enough, Satan would give up every time."

" 'Pears like ye're right," observed Socrates again.

The Load-Bearer continued, with increasing emphasis:

"I see right away the difference a-twixt Lincoln en Douglas warn't so much in Lincoln bein' a good ways over six foot en Douglas a good ways under, ez it war in thar eyes. The Jedge looked like he war speakin' agin time, but Abe Lincoln looked plumb through the meetin' into the Everlastin'—the way Moses must hev looked when he see Canaan ahead—en I kin tell ye I never did see a man look thet a-way.

"The Jedge is some pum'kins fer squeezin' hisself in, but I reckon the six-footer hez got the rulin' hand this time."

"They're at the cross-roads!" ejaculated Lem Stephens; "but them thar Abolitionists air in a howlin' wilderness, en the partin' o' the ways don't lead nowheres; thar ain't no sign-posts, not in this 'ere case. I've been lost more'n oncet by takin' the wrong road jes' when I felt dead sartin' I war on the right track. Gee whizz! I kin take ye te a place over near Edwardsville whar nothin' walkin' on two legs kin tell the difference a-twixt the p'ints o' the compass on a cloudy day; en even when the sun's a-shinin' ye've got te smell the way jes' like a hound, fer seein' don't do no good.

"I'll tell ye what it is, in this 'ere business whar politics is right on the cross-roads they want sunthin' more'n two eyes te see with. A man's got te know whar he's a-goin'. I see an Injun oncet put his ear te the groun' te tell which road te take. Arter a while he got up, give his breast a thump, en struck out ez if he war a bloodhound arter a nigger. En don't ye go te thinkin' he tuck the wrong road neither. How d'ye allow they air goin' te free the niggers? They ain't got no weepons, en the slave-owners air a sight cuter with shootin'-irons nur the Abolitionists be. Ever sence Daniel Boone settled t'other side the Ohio the white folks o' the South hev been aimin' at movin' targets—all kyinds o' birds en varmints, flyin' en runnin', includin' niggers en Injuns."

"Ez fer settin' on 'em free," said the Load-Bearer, "I ain't allowin' nothin' but God Almighty's hand; en shorely with thet comet up yander we air movin' into conflictin' times. If I hed any doubts my mind war set at rest when I heared Abe Lincoln speak; if he had jes' riz up en looked at the folks they would a-felt his power jes' the same."

"I've seen him," said Zack Caverly, "when he played mournin' tunes on their heart-strings till they mourned with the mourners."

Elihu Gest straightened himself up, and the tone of his voice changed.

"But somehow it 'peared like Abe Lincoln would hev such loads ez no man ever carried sence Christ walked in Israel. When I went over fer te hear him things looked mighty onsartin; 'peared like I hed more'n I could stand up under; but he hadn't spoke more'n ten minutes afore I felt like I never hed no loads. I begin te feel ashamed o' bein' weary en complainin'. When I went te hear him I 'lowed the Lord might let me carry some loads away, but I soon see Abe Lincoln war ekil te carry his'n en mine too, en I sot te wonderin' 'bout the workin's o' Providence."

"But ye war only listenin' to an Abolitionist a-stumpin' this hull tarnation kedentry," remarked Lem Stephens with all the bitterness he could put into the words.

"Arter all, I reckon religion en politics air 'bout the same," broke in Socrates.

"Sin in politics," answered the Load-Bearer, "air ekil te sin in religion—thar ain't no dividin' line," a remark which made Lem Stephens begin a loud and prolonged tattoo on the log with his wooden stump.

"Pete Cartwright," he blurted out, "hez allers been agin Abe Lincoln; how d'ye kyount for it?"

"I 'low Brother Cartwright hez worked a heap o' good ez a preacher," was the cool reply of Elihu Gest, "but things ain't a-goin' te be changed by preachin' alone. There'll be fire en brimstone fer some, er that blazin' star up yander don't mean nothin', en thar ain't no truth in the Scriptur's."

There were sounds as of something rushing through the underbrush and the crackling of dry timber some distance away, and when I looked in that direction I saw what seemed a faint flash of a lantern. One of the hounds under the cabin gave signs of uneasiness.

The Load-Bearer continued, lowering his voice:

"I feel like I did afore the war with Mexico, 'cept we didn't see no comet then."

"They did make a confounded fuss over thet war," observed Socrates, "en I remember Clay en Calhoun having it hot over sunthin' er nuther; both on 'em faced the music fer a reelin' breakdown. Clay sez to Calhoun: 'Ye've been expoundin' a p'int o' law I ain't never diskivered in the book o' statues. Yer argiments air shaky, en yer jedgments air ez splashy ez the Mississippi in flood-time. The hull nation's cavin' in, en thar ain't a man among ye knows 'nough te plug things up en stop the leakin'.'

"But Calhoun put the question ez peert ez a blue-jay: 'What's a-leakin'?' sez he; ' 'tain't the ship o' State, it's the whisky barrel.'

" 'Jes' so,' says Henry Clay, ez sassy ez a cat-bird in nestin' time; 'you en yer party hev knocked the plug out, but me en my party air a-goin' te double dam thet leakin'.'

"Old Hickory I see oncet at a Methodist meetin'. Pete Cartwright war a-preachin' when Old Hickory walked in. The presidin' elder sez to the preacher: 'Thet's Andrew Jackson'; but Pete Cartwright didn't noways keer. 'Who's Andrew Jackson?' he sez. 'If he's a sinner God'll damn him the same ez He would a Guinea nigger.' En he went right on preachin'."

"Thar's nothin' I despise so much ez an Abolition Methodist," ejaculated Lem Stephens. "Tar en feathers air a heap too good fer some on 'em."

This remark was evidently intended for the Load-Bearer, but he seemed not to hear.

"When ye're corn-huskin'," said Socrates, "ye put on gloves, but ye take 'em off when ye're gropin' roun' fer sinners' souls. Some preachers en politicioners take holt like they war the hounds en the people a passel o' var-mints. But a preacher thet knows what he's about allers takes the p'ints iv a meetin' like he would the p'ints iv a horse. He hez te spy out the kickers en the balky ones, en wust iv all, them thet's half mustang en half mule, en act accordin'. I 'low a man kin do a sight with flowin' words en saft soap, but ez fer the mules en cross-breeds, saft soap won't tetch 'em."

"I agree with ye thar, Brother Caverly," said the Load-Bearer; "when the meetin's anyways conflictin' it air mighty hard te deal with the Word: some wants singin', some wants preachin', en some wants prayin'."

"I reckon it air ez ye say; but ye might ez well send a retriever arter dead ducks with a tin kittle tied te his tail ez te try en land some sinners with a long string o' prayers. A man's got te roll up en wade in hisself if he wants te find them thet's been winged. When folks sets en blinks like brown owls, 'thout flappin' a wing er losin' a feather, I want te know what a pore preacher kin do! 'Tain't easy te tell who's been tetched."

"Thar's a sight o' difference a-twixt what a preacher hez te do en what a politician hez," answered Elihu Gest. "A preacher hez te wrastle with the sins o' the world every time he stands afore the people."

"Ye see," continued Zack Caverly, filling his pipe, "the 'sponsibility ain't the same. In the meetin'-house the man o' God ain't got but one kyind te wrastle with, en thet air sinners. He's arter game what cain't fly, seein' ez how they ain't angels yit; en ez they's occupyin' the floor he's 'bleeged te shoot low, allowin' the crows a-settin' on the fence to set right whar they be.

"But a politicioner's in a heap wuss fix; he's 'bleeged to deal with them what's on the fence, kase he knows the crows air jes' waitin' to see which side the fattest worms air a-comin' up on. But them thet's plumb full o' religion ain't got no room fer worms."

He lit his pipe, took a few puffs, and then went on:

"I 'low them lawyers en jedges en stump-speakers over at Springfield ain't fishin' fer snappin' turtles with nothin' but red feathers from a rooster's tail. A politicioner nowadays hez got to be ez cunnin' ez a possum thet's playin' dead, en a heap cuter'n a catamount a-layin' roun' fer the hull hog—fer if he ain't he'll be ketched hisself. Think o' the all-fired predicamints they find tharselves in! Talk about wrastlin' with sin en Satan, Elihu! Why, thar ain't a stump-meetin' but what a Republican hez te spar the Demicrats on a p'int o' law, en trip up the Know-nothin's on a question o' niggers; en while the Whigs air fannin' him with brick-bats he's mighty lucky if he ain't 'spected te hold a candle te the devil while he's a-bein' robbed o' purty nigh all his cowcumbers en water-melons en more'n half his whisky en character."

At this moment the sudden arrival of three men on horseback interrupted the conversation.

"Good evening, gentlemen," said the leader; "have you heard of any runaways about here within the last day or two?"

"I ain't heared o' none; they don't never come this way," Socrates replied.

"We're looking for three runaway slaves that are said to be somewhere in this vicinity."

" 'Bout how long hev they been out?" asked Lem Stephens.

"We lost track of them two days ago; they are somewhere near this creek."

"How many be they?"

"Two women and a boy; there's a reward of five hundred dollars."

"Let me go with ye," said Lem Stephens, hurriedly going towards his horse; "en if we don't see nothin' of 'em to-night I'll help ye find 'em in the mornin'."

After some futile words the three men and Lem Stephens wished us good-night and rode away.

By a sudden turn in the chain of events we had been brought to the verge that divides the high level of freedom from the abyss of bondage, and a feeling of distress seized hold of the company. The two men could find no words for speech. But out of the depths of the night the voices of Nature assailed them: from the woods behind us came the hooting and cries of owl and wild cat, from the prairie came tiny insects that floated past with buzzing whispers in the ears of conscience, crickets sent a thrill of warning from under the logs, tree-toads whistled near the creek, and a whip-poor-will soared and called over the cabin and the ghostly outlines of the woods.

Everything was free except the fugitives hovering somewhere near the cabin: birds and animals could roam about at will, the comet had the universe for a circuit, Socrates, in his humble cabin, was a king in his easy independence, my father, with all his cares, could go and come as he pleased, Elihu Gest, in spite of his "loads," enjoyed the freedom of the earth as far as his eyes could see or his horses carry him; and now, perhaps within a few hundred yards of us, three human beings were still panting in the throes of bondage.

But the time had come to speak, and as my father and the drover joined us the Load-Bearer said:

"It air the mother en her boy en gal. I 'low they ain't a-goin' te be separated in this world."

"Ye talk ez if ye knowed all about it," remarked Socrates; "but they'll be ketched afore to-morrer noon if they air anywhar's roun' here."

"I'm only tellin' ye my idee, en I reckon ye'll find I'm right."

The Load-Bearer walked to the other side of the cabin and stood for some moments without speaking.

"Jes' you keep still en set right whar ye be till I come back," he said, returning towards us.

He walked along the road where it bordered the woods. The three mounted men had come down this road. We all wondered what impulse could have induced him to take that direction.

The Load-Bearer had not been gone more than two or three minutes before Zack Caverly's favourite hound set up a plaintive whining under the cabin.

"Spy! Keep still thar!" said his master.

"That ole dog's got wind o' sunthin' quare," he remarked. "I've larned 'em all te keep ez still ez mice when me en other folks air about, but thar's sunthin' unusual a-gettin' ready er Spy wouldn't ez much ez sneeze. He beats all the dogs I ever hed. Thet hound *kin* smell! En ez fer hearin', I b'lieve he kin hear what's a-goin' on most anywhar's.

"But ye wouldn't think he could tell shucks from hoe-cakes, his looks air so innercent en pleadin'! He useter be the best fighter among 'em, but now he knows 'tain't wisdom te be brash.

"It took me nigh on three year te larn him the difference a-twixt wolf en b'ar, er skunk en wild cat, en all the other varmints, en thet ain't sayin' nothin' 'bout two-legged critters. Ye see, it war this a-way: I war 'bleeged te p'int te the head iv any varmint thet hed been shot er trapped, usin' only one word, en thet word meanin' the varmint; en by callin' the names over en over agin he got te know what I meant when I asked: 'Air it wolf?' 'Air it b'ar?' en so on plumb down te 'Air it nigger?' "

Socrates now called on the hound to come out.

Spy came to his master, and, looking into his face, seemed to expect some command. Socrates began:

"Air it wolf?" The dog gave no sign. "Air it b'ar?" Still no response. "Air it nigger?" The old dog gave unmistakable signs of assent.

"Them runaways ain't fur off," said Socrates; "but I ain't a-goin' te let Spy go arter 'em, he might skeer 'em away from Elihu, en he'll bring 'em in if they're alive en kickin'. If thar's anyone in this hull kintry ez know's more'n thet old hound it air Elihu Gest. He's arter loads day en night, en he ain't happy onless he's gettin' hisself into a bushel o' trouble. Ole Spy en him war clost friends from the word Go, en I reckon Elihu hez rescued more runaways than ary other Abolitionist in this deestric'; but they ain't never ketched him at it; they might ez well look fer a sow's ear in a b'ar's den."

I thought I could hear the sound of voices in the direction the Load-Bearer had gone, but I soon began to think I must have been mistaken, for not till nearly half an hour later did we hear him coming towards the cabin.

He was walking as fast as he could, with a boy in one arm and a woman leaning on the other.

"Great Jehosephat!" exclaimed Socrates; "if Elihu ain't got more'n enough fer a load. But he's mistaken 'bout thar bein' three on 'em. I 'low two's enough, sech ez they be."

Elihu Gest came full into view; even with his firm support the woman hanging on his arm was hardly able to walk. But scarcely had he put down the boy when another figure was seen approaching. It was the woman's daughter—a handsome octoroon of about seventeen—hobbling along with the aid of a crutch made from a dry branch.

"I'll be durned if he warn't right arter all," observed Socrates, hurrying into the cabin to make a fire.

"We got plenty time; them thet's scoutin' roun' these diggin's won't be back agin to-night."

The fugitives were placed on the ground, with the logs behind them as props, and the Load-Bearer asked:

" 'Bout how long air it sence ye hed any vittles?"

I could not hear the answer, but Elihu Gest exclaimed: "Three days without vittles, en all on 'em mos' dead!"

Elihu made haste with the coffee, while Socrates was hurrying with the supper.

Once in a while a groan came from the group of figures. The sound mingled with the mysteries of the surrounding darkness. It put fresh courage into the heart of the Load-Bearer, and strengthened him to assume still greater burdens. Socrates worked in silence, and during this time we were all wondering what ought to be done with the fugitives. To let them be caught was out of the question, but what to do with them after they had partaken of supper was a point that puzzled everyone. My father thought it dangerous to leave them so near the cabin.

To the great relief of all, the drover mounted his horse

and rode away, perhaps not wishing to become involved in any responsibility and to steer clear of a situation which might compromise him in the eyes of the law.

"Looky here," remarked Zack Caverly to the Load-Bearer, "ye don't reckon he's goin' over Lem Stephens's way, do ye?"

"I don't reckon he air; 'pears like he allers turns off thar by Ebenezer Hicks's cornfield."

The coffee was ready and the Load-Bearer and Socrates were serving it out in the big blue china cups which we had used at our supper—the bacon and hoe-cakes would soon follow.

Every moment now seemed like an hour.

My father, Elihu, and Socrates went into the cabin to talk over the affair and decide on what to do.

They were coming out of the cabin when the drover returned bringing the news that the slave-catchers had decided to pay Socrates another visit that night.

It did not take long for the Load-Bearer to come to a decision. He called for aid, and one by one the three runaways were lifted into his wagon.

"Whar be ye goin', Elihu? They've seed ye here, en ye'll be called on shore en sartin."

"I don't know no more'n you; but I ain't a-goin' te stop till God Almighty tells me."

He drove off into the night, taking the road to the east. We followed on the same road shortly after, but met no one on the way home. When we arrived at the Log-House we found that it, too, had been visited by the slave-hunters.

Chapter VII

At the Post-Office

ONE morning I went with my father to the post-office, which was in a small store by the railway station, about six miles distant.

How bleak and forsaken it was! The place consisted of two houses and some freight cars shunted off the main line. The prairie here had a desolate look, but to the north lay a wooded district, and here my father brought me to stand on a small embankment to watch the train coming up around a curve out of the woods.

The sight made an impression that was lasting, for at this moment it is just as vivid as it was then. It made my nerves tingle and opened the door to a new world of wonders. The train itself, filled with passengers, did not interest me: it was the engine, with its puffing steam, its cow-catcher, and its imposing smoke-stack, that possessed the attraction.

The day soon came, however, when the locomotive took the second place in my imagination and the passengers the first. What, after all, was the steam-engine compared with human beings, animals, and birds? What was its smoke and movement compared with pictures of earth, sky, and water? At rest, the locomotive ceased to interest; but the aspect of the world was always changing. A landscape had its four seasons. Every manifestation of Nature harmonised with some mood or condition of the mind, and I watched the buzzards and bluebirds, the cranes and chick-a-dees, the rabbits and squirrels, with renewed and ever-increasing interest. Nature changed, but never grew stale. The air was full of song and colour, the earth full of forms and movement, and the rapid motion of a garter-snake was, after all, more fascinating than the movement of an engine with its train of cars; and how could the noise of the puffing compare with a chorus of red-winged black-birds? Nature is the one perennial charm.

But this was not the opinion of poor Monsieur Duval, one of the unfortunate settlers who had mistaken the wilderness for a ready-made paradise. All the loungers at the post-office looked like members of the same family excepting this Frenchman and a German settler whom they called "Dutchy." Duval resembled a shipwrecked mariner among the inhabitants of some remote island, the secret of whose language and customs he could not fathom. But he and the German were full of life, while the others seemed too listless and lazy to do more than whittle sticks and once in a while hit a certain spot by an expectoration of tobacco-juice.

The scene was set off by rows of tea-canisters, coffee-sacks, bolts of calico, sugar-barrels, bacon, rice, and plug-tobacco, with sundry farming implements stored at the back, and a few pigeon-holes for letters.

The shuffling figure of the goateed proprietor stood in the midst of all, a little taller and perhaps a little more languid than any of the others, too indifferent to talk, yet putting in a word now and again mechanically without stopping to calculate the effect of what he said and without being interested in any person or thing. He aroused my interest as soon as he said to my father:

"Wal, I'm going to wind her up—goin' to vamose."

"Going to leave us?"

"Ya-as," he drawled; "goin' to wind up and move on."

A man sitting on the edge of a large box, half-filled with empty sacks, called out:

"Which a-way?"

"Over to Pike Kyounty," was the answer.

The Frenchman, who was standing against the counter, straightened up.

"Me, too," he exclaimed, tapping his bosom once for each word, "me, too, I wind her up, I go vamose."

"Goin' to sell out, too?"

"If I no sell heem I geef heem 'way," he answered with a gesture of supreme disgust.

"How long have you been here?" asked the store-keeper.

"Two, tree year."

"Hardly long enough to give the country a fair trial," said my father.

"Try heem! I geef him plenty tam. Ze farm he try me lak Job was try wiz hees sheep an' hees camelle!"

"Have you had much illness?"

"Do I look seek? My wife, my son, meself, we work lak niggair. We haf no tam for eat, no tam for sleep, no tam for wash ourself."

"You must have taken up too much land. Most of the trouble comes from that."

"No, monsieur, we no haf too much, but we been too much for ze land."

"I suppose you are from some part of the South?"

"Me, I come from New Orleans. I haf one big family; I lose heem wiz ze yellow fevair. My friends say, 'You go up ze Mississippi, you 'scape ze fevair.' I tak my wife an' son to Saint-Louis. Someone say, 'You tak one farm in Illinois, ze soil she been so rich you scratch heem two, tree tam wiz hoe, everyzing come up while you look!' Wen I come on ze farm ze soil she been too hard for scratch; I get one plough, so long, for cut ze bit root, an four pair ox for pool her. But ze wild cat come in ze night; she clam up ze tree an' tak ze turkey; ze fox brak in ze hen-house an' tak ze chicken. In ze morning I find ze haid an' some feddair."

He stopped to consider a moment, then continued: "I keep some bee for mak bees' wax. I go look—I find ze hive sprawl on ze groun'; zey haf left me nozzing!"

"What animal do you suppose it was?"

"Tell me, monsieur, do ze fox lak for eat ze bee? Do ze wild cat lak for chew ze bees' wax? Do ze mink lak for haf her nose sting? Ah, monsieur, I lak for someone tell me zat!"

Duval gave a fierce look at the man sitting on the box, for he had just fallen over on the sacks in a spasm of laughter, his feet in the air, and we concluded he could tell what had become of the Frenchman's bees if he chose.

"But zat is not ze worst," he went on. "One tam I haf ver' good crop. Ze corn, ze legume, ze poomkin, she been all plant an' come up. But ze army-worm she come! Next day I go look—she leave me nozzing but ze cobble-stone."

Then, as if he had forgotten something, he added:

"Ze cow come home an' I go for milk her—she been dry lak my old boot; ze worm haf eat her foddair!"

He let his arms fall in a limp gesture of resignation, and taking from his pocket a cheap cigar, and leaning with one arm on the counter, he began smoking, letting out great puffs through his nose as if in this way he were getting rid of all the evil things connected with pioneer life.

The hang-dog faces of the men sitting and lolling about were enlivened by grins, and ironical remarks were freely indulged in.

"Say, Frenchy," said the man sitting on the box, "what'll ye take te hire out jes' te keep away b'ars en' skunks?"

Duval gave the man one contemptuous look. Evidently he was not going to answer. He smoked while he walked carelessly towards the box, and when within a few feet of it made a sudden, cat-like bound at the man, clutching his throat with the grip of a frenzied gorilla while he forced him down into the box head foremost.

The onlookers, stunned by the suddenness of the attack, seemed dazed and helpless, staring at the scene as if held by some horrible fascination. Then a gurgling sound came from the victim, causing someone to cry out:

"I'll be hanged if he ain't chokin' him to death!"

"I'm durned if he ain't!" exclaimed someone else.

"Haul him off!" shouted the store-keeper, roused out of his lethargy; "we don't want no dead men round here!"

The store-keeper, assisted by one of the man's friends,

began to tug at the Frenchman. Hardly had they done so when a man with a knife made a rush for Duval; but the "Dutchman" was waiting his chance; he felled him to the floor by one quick blow from his great, open hand, the hard, thick palm and huge, long fingers making a splitting noise like a blade of steel on a sheet of ice.

"No! By sheemany!" he growled, as he picked up the knife and shook it in their faces. "You don't come dem games here! Ven you gif me dat shifferee I hef some buckshot ready, but mine vife she don't let me shoot nodding. Now I gif you someding mit interest," and with that he brought the same open hand down on the man who had helped to pull Duval off his victim. He fell to the floor as if struck with a mallet, and I shuddered, for he seemed to be stone dead. This was the third surprise within a few seconds. The man in the box was not yet able to rise to his feet, but Duval was looking about him ready for more work and well inclined to keep it going. His eyes were bloodshot and his face was all afire. He stood like some ferocious animal in the arena ready for any opponent, with a firm faith in his two hands, his two legs, his nimble body and his quick wit, while the "Dutchman" had good reason to pin his faith to a pair of broad palms, which resembled the paws of a bear in thickness, and a body unimpaired by fiery whisky and malarial fever.

Two of the gang were now placed *hors de combat*, and this without the use of knives or firearms. It was now four against two, and the Frenchman had evidently summed up the situation at a glance; with a quick, twisting movement he turned his body like a practised wrestler, and the man standing beside him found himself sprawling on the floor, his feet knocked from under him by the deft manœuvres of Duval's foot.

All was now over. After this the gang resembled nothing so much as a pack of whipped dogs, and the stillness that reigned in the store had something of the stillness of the battlefield after the fury of the battle.

Duval and the "Dutchman" left the store together and became close friends from that day.

Chapter VIII

My Visit to the
Load-Bearer's Home

MY MOTHER was busy getting ready for another baking. She had baked the day before, and I could not help wondering what all the extra bread was for.

I had not long to wait for an answer to my thoughts: she stopped in the middle of her work, cleaned the rolling-pin of dough, and went to the pantry, where she stood and looked for some moments at the things inside.

"Oh, dear!" she said, with one of her gentle sighs which I always understood so well; "there is not much, but what there is must go to-day, and in a day or two I shall send more."

Out came all the bread and the meat and a pound of coffee, with sugar. These were stored away in the saddle-bags, for she said it was too far to walk and I would have to saddle my pony.

"But where to?" I asked with surprise.

"To Mrs. Gest's; these things are for her."

"The Load-Bearer married!" I exclaimed.

"Why, of course he's married, like all good Christians," she observed, smiling; "and you'll be married too, some day, when the proper time comes."

I had pictured him as a kind of hermit, living somewhere all alone, perhaps being fed by ravens, like Elijah the prophet; and even now I could hardly believe that he had a regular, fixed abode.

I was to tell Mrs. Gest she could count on my mother's aid when she had "visitors from the South," which meant fugitive slaves trying to reach Canada.

The affair at the cabin of Socrates had been discussed between my parents, and this was the result.

No member of the family had ever been to the home of Elihu Gest. We knew he lived near a large creek, some four or five miles south-west of the meeting-house; so off I went in the full belief that I would find the place by asking here and there on the way.

The country beyond the meeting-house was like another world to me. The prairie, the dim outline of the woods beyond, the atmosphere, all combined to produce a sense of freshness and novelty, and the effect on my mind could not have been greater had I gone a hundred miles from home.

After riding what seemed to me a long distance a man in a wagon directed me to a road bordering a strip of wood which led into a region of trees and underbrush, with patches of prairie here and there, and vistas of the creek and the undulating ground beyond. The land had a gentle slope towards the water. The beech trees rose to a great height, and now and then, through an opening in the woods, I could see a distance of two miles; but in most places the world all around was hidden by rocky knobs, thick underbrush, and immense trees.

"What a place to hide in!" I thought; and I was beginning to fear my search for the house would not end in success, when I heard the barking of a dog some considerable distance to the left. Stopping to consider what to do, I detected faint tracks of wagon wheels leading in that direction. I followed as best I could over a parterre of leaves, moss, and the *débris* of decayed timber.

Penetrating still farther, I came upon a clearing, and then I caught a glimpse of a small frame house almost hidden by trees and shrubs. As I approached, three savage dogs, which I at first took to be wolves, chained up, began a fierce barking and howling. As I was about to get off my pony and ask if Elihu Gest lived here, a thin, pale-faced woman, her hair streaked with grey, opened the door. Then, wiping her mouth with her apron, she exclaimed:

"Bless ye, sonny, ye ain't come with bad news, hev ye? My ole man's been gone two full days en nights!"

It was Cornelia Gest, the Load-Bearer's wife.

I told her who had sent me and what I had brought; but it did not allay her anxiety when I recounted the incidents at the cabin of Socrates.

"Git right down en come in, en tell me all about it," she said; "I 'spect ye need a rest. It allers makes my head ache ridin' over the prairie in the hot sun."

I got off the pony, and after tying up took the things into the kitchen.

"Land! How good yer ma is," she exclaimed, "sendin' me all these things in case o' needcessity. Elihu told me 'bout her. Some folks don't need te hev wings te be angels. How did yer ma know I hedn't but one loaf o' bread left? It do beat all how things work out! I 'lowed te do some bakin' to-day, but somehow I couldn't git te work. 'Pears like when Elihu's away en I don't know his whereabouts I cain't git nothin' done! Law me! if here ain't coffee! Elihu ain't never ceased talkin' 'bout yer ma's coffee. What does she cl'ar it with?"

All this time I was wondering what she would do if her husband should fail to return before evening.

"I'm right glad ye've come te cher a body; the hours air longer when ye're mos' dead worryin'. When he stayed away afore he 'lowed he wouldn't hev time te git back, en I warn't noways afeared he'd got hisself into trouble."

There was something in her voice and look that aroused my sympathy.

"I set up all las' night prayin' en readin' in the Good Book," she went on; "'twarn't in mortal natur' te sleep."

She seemed far away in thought. Her eyes were fixed on the floor, and I began to ask myself why everyone had so much trouble. As I only sat and listened she had become unconscious of my presence in the house; but after a while she straightened up and resumed:

"I recken he tuck the runaways over te Uriah Busby's, en from there he'll take 'em on te the nex' station."

She mused for a time again, and then continued:

"But it ain't easy; the resks air turrible; but then, ez Elihu sez, when the Lord en His hosts air with ye thar ain't no call te feel skeered. Elihu en Ike Snedeker en Ebenezer Carter en Tom Melendy, they don't none o' them know what it air te fail."

After sitting for some time without speaking she suddenly clasped her hands and rose from her seat, and stretching out her thin, bare arms, with trembling body and quivering lips, her voice went up in a long, loud wail:

"Lord, help a pore fersaken woman! Help me this day, fer my troubles air more'n I kin bear without Ye. Make it so I kin set here alone without repinin'; send Elihu home, oh my Lord en my God, fer I cain't live without him."

Her look appalled me. I saw grief manifest in words and gesture. . . . I pictured to myself my mother pleading with the Eternal. I imagined what the Log-House would be with my father absent and his whereabouts unknown.

How I wished to say something comforting to the lonely woman standing there, but I, who could never express to my mother what I thought and felt when she was in trouble, could not find words to comfort a stranger. I was overcome with a pity and sympathy which I was powerless to express, and I wondered what would become of the little home in the woods if the Load-Bearer never returned. It seemed as if I had known this house and its occupants all my life, that we were in some way closely related.

I proposed to ride over to the Busbys for any news I could gather there. It would take about an hour and a half. But we could arrive at no decision, and I was thinking of returning when we saw Elihu Gest slowly wending his way home through the most unfrequented part of the woods. He had followed the creek a good part of the way, and his wagon seemed full of farming implements and sacks of grain.

Cornelia Gest stood at the door awaiting his arrival.

"Fer the land's sake!" she ejaculated when he got within talking distance, "whar hev ye been?"

She paused a moment and then continued:

"I don't know whether I'm looking right at ye er whether it's yer ghost a-drivin' them hosses. How d'ye 'low I've been settin' here two endurin' nights through without ye?"

"Now, Cornely," he pleaded, "don't ye take on so. When I tell ye all about it ye'll be s'prised en mighty glad I didn't come right home from the post-office. But I want ye te help me unload right here, fer it don't matter whar we set these things."

We all went to work. The implements, or what I took to be such, were soon placed on the ground, but the sacks, instead of containing grain or potatoes, were filled with straw. We lifted off those nearest the dash-board, the Load-Bearer flung back a horse-blanket, and three faces, frightened, haggard, and woe-begone, looked out from the hay underneath. It was the quadroon mother and her two octoroon children.

"White folks!" gasped Cornelia, stunned by the unexpected.

"I 'low the two air white enough, more's the pity," assented Elihu.

"Goodness me! Elihu Gest!" protested Cornelia when the two stepped into the kitchen; "we ain't got no place fer white folks. Thar's plenty vittles, but we ain't got no room, ye know we ain't; en two on 'em look like they hedn't but one more breath te let out en they war holdin' on to it till they got here."

"Wal, now," he said, "jes' give me a leetle time te let out *my* breath, fer me, too, I've been holdin' it in ever sence night afore last."

But she persisted:

"Whar on the face o' this yearth hev ye fished out sech a load? Ye ain't never carried home nothin' te ekil it! Whar *hev* ye been? Do tell!"

"Why, ain't Bub here told ye?"

"He told me 'bout three runaways ye found over at Zack Caverly's, two on 'em mos' dead."

"Jes' so, en I driv 'em te brother Busby's, whar I war obleeged te wait fer a good chance te git away, en now they air in the wagon thar."

Cornelia sank into a seat. Amazement and indignation were depicted on every feature. Her jaws were firmly set and I could hear her teeth grate.

"White slaves!" she groaned. "I know ye ain't given te jokes, Elihu, but I cain't git it into my head how thar kin be slaves thet air ez white ez we be; somehow I couldn't never believe it; but accordin' te your tellin' I've got te believe it, and now I've seen it with my own eyes."

She did not seem like the woman who, a short time before, was complaining of her sorrows and tribulations. Indignation had given way to a desire to act, to help, to save the lives of the fugitives and send them on their way towards Canada.

"I war calc'latin' te bring 'em in the house," remarked the Load-Bearer, as the two left the kitchen and walked over to the wagon, "but I reckon it air safer to take 'em te the barn. Thar'll be a mite iv a chance thet if anyone comes arter 'em they won't go te the barn te look."

"Wal," agreed Cornelia, "thar ain't no objections te clean, new hay fer beds, en we kin take some things over from the house."

"To-morrer I'll hev te step about en find a new hidin'-place, fer I heared another band o' runaways air summars south o' here, en they may be along afore we know it."

"Don't ye go te doin' too much all te oncet," interposed his wife, "er ye'll be ailin' en things 'll be a sight wuss."

"To-morrer I'll take 'em te the cave by the creek. I 'lowed te hev it all fixed afore now, but things hev come about mighty sudden. Thet cave needs a heap o' fixin'. I ain't hed no sleep fer two nights en I skasely know what I'm a-doin'."

For the first time I took notice of the Load-Bearer's tired face. His eyes expressed the hope and faith which inspired him, but a great weariness made his walk heavy and his movements slow.

It was all Elihu and Cornelia Gest could do to get the eldest of the two women out of the wagon and into the barn. There was enough to keep all hands busy. I ran to and fro with blankets and pillows, while Mrs. Gest attended to the immediate wants of the fugitives.

When I had done all I could at the barn and returned to the house I found Socrates standing close to the Load-Bearer's dogs. He was evidently in one of his keenest talking moods:

"Ye kin kyount on what I'm tellin' ye," he was saying. "I hev fit varmints my hull life, en hev teached dogs, en I hev fed 'em so ez te make 'em win. Mebbe ye'll be in fer a fight afore long, en ye cain't keep 'em chained 'thout hevin' 'em fall off some en git sorter limp in the fore-legs—reecollect a dog fights ez much with his legs ez he does with his teeth. If Lem Stephens's bloodhounds come nosin' up this way ye'll be in fer a lively kick-up."

"I've been wonderin' how ye keep yer dogs so sleek and spry," remarked the Load-Bearer. "What d'ye feed 'em on? Any pertickler kyind o' meat?"

"Give 'em mos' anythin' but liver, en let 'em run roun' consider'ble. But tie 'em up en starve 'em fer a day er so afore ye calc'late te use 'em fer any fightin'."

Zack Caverly was eyeing with extraordinary interest the three huge wolf-hounds, whose cold, agate eyes conjured up in my imagination images of the haunts of wolf and bear and the cruel romance of wold and wilderness. Compared with the Load-Bearer's dogs the hounds at the cabin of Socrates were the incarnation of docility and affection.

The wolf-hounds gave us a look now and then of glacial indifference. There was no caressing to be indulged in here, no patting on the back, no words of encouragement expected or needed. I could not distinguish any difference between them—they all looked the same height, colour, and size—but the Load-Bearer knew the characteristics of each.

As I looked at these wolf-hounds, and then at the meek, compassionate face of Elihu Gest, I was struck with the incongruity of the scene: the dogs all ferocity, the man all meekness. But from that moment I saw the Load-Bearer in a new light. Under the humane countenance there dwelt the inflexible will, the inexorable determination to dare and to do. How different he was now, standing beside his wolf-hounds, from what he looked on his first visit to the Log-House! The benevolent look was still there, but the vague, dreamy expression was gone, and in its place appeared a realisation of present responsibilities. Plotting and planning had taken the place of dreams.

"They don't need no coddlin'," observed Socrates, as he eyed them one after the other, slowly and critically. "I ain't seed no dog-flesh ekil to 'em sence I war down in Tennessee, en if ye treat 'em ez I say ye'll hev good reason te be thankful, Elihu."

"The Lord made 'em, Brother Caverly, en they air here accordin' te His will, en I'm right glad ye see thar p'ints air p'ints te reckon on."

"I ain't seed thar ekil," he declared, giving the Load-Bearer a knowing look; "they're ez full o' p'ints ez a porcupine air o' quills, en I reckon it ain't no ways discommodin' fer a man in your cirkinstances te hev sech pets layin' roun', jes' pinin' away kase thar ain't no live meat fer te clean thar teeth on."

" 'Pears like they ain't got no feelin's, 'ceptin' fer huntin' en fightin'," remarked Elihu, contemplating the animals much as he would so many savage Indians.

"They don't show no pertikler likin' fer anybody," returned Socrates; "but ye'll allow a good wagger makes a pore watcher, en some on 'em gits more'n enough te eat by not knowin' they hev tails."

"If thar ain't Sister Busby!" exclaimed the Load-Bearer, as Serena emerged from the woods on a big, slow, floundering sorrel.

Elihu Gest seemed ill at ease when he saw her coming. She came like a rain-cloud, and her presence threw a cold douche over all. Serena Busby's tongue was all the more dangerous because her intentions were good and every-body liked her, but she was apt to tell the gravest secrets without being conscious of what she was saying.

"Where's Cornely?" she shouted, before the sorrel came to a stop at the kitchen door.

"I've brought ye over some b'ars' grease en camphire," she went on as she caught sight of Mrs. Gest coming from the barn. "I forgot all about it this mornin' when Elihu left, everyone bein' so flustered."

"How good ye be!" said Cornelia. "I war sayin' to Elihu jes' now thet we hedn't nothin' in the house to rub with, en the gal's ankle do need 'tendin' to. Ez fer gittin' a doctor, 'tain't no use thinkin' o' sech a thing. Thar ain't no one 'cept Doc. Reed in Jacksonville we could trust to keep the secret, en he's too fur away."

"This is what we all use fer sprains en bruises," replied Serena. "Ye know she ain't hed no bones broke. It all come about by havin' te jump over logs like rabbits with hounds after 'em that night when the slave-hunters were on thar tracks. It's horrible te see the poor thing suffer so! But her mother is plumb used up; she wouldn't taste a mite o' vittles over to my house, en I tried her with everything. Sakes alive!" she exclaimed, putting her hand into a deep pocket and taking out a small parcel, "I mos' forgot the tea; it's *green* tea, Cornely—some that Uriah got the last time he was down to Alton, en if *that* don't make her set up nothin' will. It'll give her backbone. But law! ain't the children white! It was the boy's curly hair made me think o' runaways, but I declare I'd take 'em fer white folks if they was dressed up real nice."

"I didn't take no pertickler notice the night Elihu dis-

kivered 'em," observed Socrates, "en I ain't seed 'em sence
—not te look squar' at 'em."

Cornelia Gest had no more to say. She pretended a deep
interest in the things Mrs. Busby had brought, but her
mind was elsewhere. Her face looked what she felt.

"Aint ye goin' te git off en stop a spell, Sister Busby?"
inquired the Load-Bearer, with bland apathy.

"Yes, do," said his wife; "shorely ye ain't goin' back
'thout seein' whar we've put 'em. We've done the best
we could; it's a sight cleaner'n some beds I've slept in
afore now."

"I promised Uriah te be right back without tyin' up,
but I'll git off en make 'em a real nice cup o' this here
tea, en we'll take it over to 'em."

"They've hed coffee," observed Cornelia, with an effort to be polite and as a mild protest against green tea.

The two women went into the kitchen, and I heard the
Load-Bearer remark:

"Sister Busby's got a sight o' hoss sense, but she do need
the bridle now and agin."

"Sereny's jes' like a skittish yearling," commented Socrates; "but don't ye go te bridlin' her tongue er she'll take
the bit 'twixt her teeth en a prairie fire won't head her
off. Give her plenty tetherin' groun' en plenty fac's te
nibble on, but don't let her chaw too close te the stumps."

"Ye kin lead a filly te the trough, Brother Caverly, but
ye cain't make her drink more'n jes' so much. Some folks
air allers thirstin' fer water from other folks's wells, but
nothin' but a runnin' stream o' gossip will slake Sister
Busby's thirst fer more knowledge."

"Thet's a fac', thet's a fac'; but the wust is the stream runs squar' through your diggin's."

"Ez things are goin' now, Sereny knows 'nough te want te know a heap more. I'm plumb with ye when ye tell me not to let her nibble till she comes to the cobble-stones."

The tea was soon made, for Mrs. Gest had kept the fire going and the water hot.

No sooner had she and Mrs. Busby disappeared into the barn than Alek Jordan came galloping up by the shortest cut from the main road.

"Marm told me te give ye this," he said to the Load-Bearer, handing him a letter; "it's from Isaac Snedeker; he give it te marm te send."

Elihu opened and read, while Zack Caverly stood and waited for the news.

The Load-Bearer heaved a sigh:

"Brother Snedeker sez he's a-comin' here to-morrer night with eight runaways."

"Whoop-ee!" exclaimed Socrates.

Then a thought struck him.

"Looky here, Alek," he said, "you jes' light out ez quick ez ever ye kin; thar's some un at the barn thet mustn't know ye've been here. Don't ye wait a minnit; take the trail through the woods by the creek ez fur ez ye kin er mebbe the runaways 'll git ketched."

The Load-Bearer had his eyes fixed on the barn, expecting every moment to see Mrs. Busby emerge and then ride part of the way home with Alek Jordan, when more than one secret would be revealed concerning the intentions of Isaac Snedeker.

Alek, whose horse was young and in fine condition, was off at a bound, the animal clearing like a buck every obstacle in his path.

Hardly had he got out of sight when Serena Busby made her appearance, followed by Cornelia Gest, who, weary and distracted, let the visitor do all the talking.

Chapter IX

A Night of Mystery

O N CERTAIN evenings my father would sit before the big, open fireplace and watch with unalloyed satisfaction the burning logs. He would see pictures in the blazing wood, and he had a science of his own in the mingling of different logs.

"How well that dried hickory burns with the damp walnut!" he would say, taking the tongs and shifting the pieces, now a little more to the front, now a little farther back.

He taught me to see castles, people, and faces in the flames and embers, and I knew what colours to expect from the different woods. He kept some that were full of sap, that would burn slowly; others were split up to dry. While sitting before the fire on a clear, bracing night my father was wont to forget every care and abandon himself to the pure pleasures of the hearth. He would dream of the past, of friends in the old country, and more than once he would remark to me, taking the tongs and pointing: "There's a face that reminds me of poor So-and-so." He loved to revisit the old familiar scenes while the fire gave them momentary life and set them before him in frames of gold and flaming opal. Then he would tell me stories of the wild animals of the old homestead, of the tracks of the marten in the snow, and how he discovered its hiding-place; of a memorable fox hunt when one of his friends held the fox up by the tail and another friend cried out from a distance: "Don't hurt the fox! don't hurt the fox!" and of his sojourn in Paris during the reign of Louis Philippe.

At such times my mother added a spirit of cheerfulness by some joyful exclamation, such as: "There's a letter in the candle!" as if the simple expression in itself would assist the arrival of good news from afar; and when I looked I saw a large flaming blob, on the side of the wick, pointing toward us.

I cannot remember whether the letters arrived, as the candle so often announced; but how vividly I recollect the nights when I lay awake in the next room and heard my parents discuss the uncertainty of the future, the imminent need of funds to carry on the work of the farm, and the possibility of failure and ruin! Such conversations occurred after the other members of the family had gone to bed, but I heard everything, and night after night I listened to these talks, and racked my brain, wondering how it would all end. My distress was even greater than that of my mother, for she knew what I did not, and she could still hope.

After such talks the quivering song of the cricket dotted the stillness with an accent of deeper melancholy, while the heavy pendulum slowly measured out the minutes between midnight and the dismal twilight of dawn.

We were all sitting quietly together the evening after my visit to the Load-Bearer's home, my mother with the

Bible in her lap—the only book she ever read while in the Log-House—my father reading a newspaper containing an account of a recent speech by Abraham Lincoln. My mother's face looked paler and more pensive than usual, for, some days previous to this, my father had had a misunderstanding with one of the settlers. The only weapon in the house was a double-barrelled gun, and even this stood unloaded against the wall in a corner of the sitting-room. No dog was kept on the place, for the reason that a dog was regarded as one of the things most likely to cause trouble with the neighbours.

The wind was blowing across the prairie from the east. My mother seemed apprehensive, and I must have caught some of the thoughts which filled her mind with gloomy presentiments. During a lull of the wind a sound reached us from the prairie. It might have been a shout or a call. How vividly it all comes before me now! She looked inquiringly at my father, who was absorbed in his newspaper and heard nothing. I needed no words to tell me what she was thinking; her face assumed a grave and anxious look. I was hoping the sound might be nothing more than the noise of belated travellers passing on horseback, when we heard it again, like a confused, mumbling menace—this time a little nearer, still disguised in the muffled wind. She walked into the next room, greatly agitated, but instantly returned and began to read in the prayer-book.

My father had just put aside his newspaper when a low, hollow murmur came from the prairie.

"What can it be?" asked my mother in a voice scarcely audible. Without answering, he went into the next room for the ammunition, took the gun from the corner and began to load with buckshot. It seemed to me he had never looked so tall, so grim, so determined as when he rammed the wadding down with the ramrod. Then he went to the front door and listened. My mother sat with closed eyes like one in a trance, until it seemed to me as if by some unaccountable hocus-pocus we had been thrust into a world where pantomime and mystery had taken the place of speech, and we were waiting for some sudden and terrible stroke of destiny. What was going to happen? Was it the end of all things at the Log-House?

My father decided not to go out by the front way, and after the light was removed he opened the kitchen door and stood outside in the dark.

"The moon is just rising," said my mother in a half-whisper, looking through the window of the front room. Then I looked, and as the clouds drifted by I saw the moon in the shape of a gleaming scythe. A sudden chill of autumn had come to the house. She hurried out to beg my father to come in, but he was creeping from corner to corner and from tree to tree, with the gun held before him, cocked and ready for that deadly aim for which he was so well known.

After going as far as the smoke-house and waiting there some time, he returned; he thought the sounds must have been due to some prowling animal. He was about to give up further search when the moaning was again heard, out a little beyond the trees, and then, as my mother stood trembling at the door, a voice shouted:

"Don' shoot, massa; don' shoot! fer de Lawd's sake don' ye shoot!"

My father went straight towards the voice.

"We done lost, massa," someone shouted as soon as he reached the open; "we is lookin' fer Massa Gest's place."

"Come in, come in."

My father came back into the kitchen with two negro fugitives.

"Where have you been?"

"Mass' Snedeker done drap us ober dere," said one of the negroes, pointing west.

"He was running you off?"

"Yes, massa."

"And finding he was chased, let you down, and so you got lost?"

"Yes, massa."

Just then a loud knocking at the front door came with terrible suddenness, for during the talk and confusion no one had heard any noise in the road.

My father took his gun, and standing at one side of the door asked who was there.

"Isaac Snedeker," answered a familiar voice.

Open went the door and in rushed Ike Snedeker, one of the most intrepid souls that ever risked death for the sake of conscience.

A man stood before us who had never known fear. One glance at this face would be enough to make an enemy stop and think twice before coming to close quarters with such a being. He was courage incarnate, with the shaggy head of a lion, the sharp, invincible eye of an eagle, the frame of an athlete, the earnestness of a convinced reformer. His hair stood out thick and bushy, and his bearded face, with the upper lip clean-shaven, gave to the whole countenance a massive, formidable look that inspired every fugitive with confidence and struck fear into the hearts of his secret foes.

"I've lost two runaways," he said, as he walked through to the kitchen; "had to let them out of the wagon over there near the maple grove—we were.followed."

"I think they are here," said my father, "and I came near shooting one of them by mistake."

"I directed them to come this way as near as I could, hoping they would strike through the prairie at this place."

My mother was now bringing the fugitives something to eat when Isaac Snedeker said peremptorily:

"Come along, it's now or never. We've got to get to Brother Gest's with that load before midnight. You see, I've had to gather 'em up here and there in different places, and I have in the wagon out there two lots—one sent over by Ebenezer Carter and the other by Brother Wolcott. If we get caught it'll be the first time; but they'd get a haul that would amount to something—I've got fourteen altogether."

The two fugitives left without having time to drink a cup of coffee, and we all went to the road to see them off. The wagon was full of frightened, trembling runaways: negroes, mulattoes, octoroons. Not a moment was lost. Isaac Snedeker had only to speak to his horses—a fine, powerful team—to send them going at a great speed down the road towards the appointed meeting-place at Elihu Gest's.

We went back into the house, where my mother sank exhausted into a rocking-chair.

But she had still another ordeal to go through. Prayers had been said, and we were all about to retire for the night, when the noise of galloping horses and men talking could be heard in the road. One moment of suspense followed another. Footsteps were heard near the kitchen door, then there came a light and somewhat timid rapping as if the persons outside were not certain about this being the right place. My father opened, this time without asking who was there. Two disreputable-looking men stood before him, one of them scowling at us through the door like some ferocious animal. They carried pistols and dirks. Their eyes were shaded by slouched hats that partly concealed the upper part of their faces, so that, for all we knew, they might have been neighbours living at no great distance from the Log-House.

"Hev ye seen any runaways hangin' round hyar?" asked the elder man, looking up from under his hat, and with an expression that told of a fearful admixture of malicious cunning and moral cowardice.

"I have," answered my father. "Who delegated you to look for them?"

The fellow hesitated. Then he stammered:

"Be you a fire-eatin' Abolitionist?"

"I have voted for Abraham Lincoln once, if that is what you mean by being an Abolitionist."

"Ye ain't been long in this country," observed the younger man.

"Long enough to become an American citizen, and vote."

This surprised them. They looked confused, but they braced themselves for a final effort.

"We're arter them runaways, en we don't calc'late te leave hyar without takin' 'em along."

"They went from here some time ago, so you'll have to look elsewhere if you want to find them."

"Let's go over to the barn," said the elder of the two.

They started for the barn, but stopped just beyond the big locust tree, and I heard the words:

"Say, Jake, I don't like the look o' that old Britisher."

"No more do I."

"He'll shoot the fust thing we know. He's got sunthin' mighty juberous in thet eye o' his'n."

Not another word was said. They wheeled about, made for the road, mounted their horses, and were off.

They had been cowed and disarmed by my father's coolness, his independence, by his towering height, and a scorn that was withering to the two slave-hunting villains.

Chapter X

Sowing and Reaping

THE wide strip of prairie to the west of the Log-House was now ready for planting, but not without immense labour. A huge plough which descended into the primitive soil was drawn by four or five pairs of stout oxen, driven and directed by a man with a whip as long as the team itself. My father held the plough, and frequently stood on it in order to drive it deep enough to cut through the roots that were often formidable in their thickness.

Oh, the delightful souvenirs of that ploughing and planting! The odour of the fresh, rich soil, never broken till now, the turning up of snakes, insects, and queer stones, with here and there the rough flint-head of an Indian arrow, the flocks of red-winged blackbirds settling down to feast in the wavy sods, the excitement which had in it no reaction—how is it possible that such things pass as in dreams?

The whole day I followed the oxen, never growing weary of the wonders of Nature, and when this rough piece of land had been ploughed, harrowed, and duly prepared for the first crop of Indian corn (maize), then came what was, to me, the climax of the whole proceedings, the actual sowing of the seed. It was like some rare holiday, a festival, a celebration. All Nature seemed to partake of the joy; a new world of marvels seemed to be on the eve of consummation. The weather was perfect, and as we three—my father, one of my sisters, and myself —went forth with a sack of seed, we dropped the large golden grains into the proper places all along through the soft, dark loam, closing up each hole, keeping up a ceaseless chatter, mainly, I think, about the pure delights of the work we were doing.

Perhaps never since have I felt the same kind of thrill. There are days that shine out like great white jewels in the crown of years.

After the planting there was little to be done except watching and waiting. We watched the sprouting of the corn till it grew through the first period. Its second period was one of flowing, silky tassels, clear and pure, with a silvery sheen, the whole field decked in opulent hangings that waved in the wind and sparkled in the sun, the stalks rising in places to a height of ten feet or more. The third period came about August, when the ripening began. It was slow, the stalks turning to a light, faded gold, the big ears hanging in heavy clusters and in countless numbers, one rivalling another in length and size. And the field now afforded another pleasure—that of getting lost in its mysterious depths. It was a happy feeding-ground for birds and a hiding-place for wild animals.

Then came two later stages—the cutting and stacking. The cutting was rough work. It was done by hired hands; and when the corn was stacked the field assumed another air, and the face of Nature thereabouts was changed beyond recognition. The stacks resembled innumerable huts or wigwams, and this was not without a charm of its own, for it made the surroundings less lonely-looking; but when the ears of corn were taken from the stalks and the field stripped bare the view was one of vacant desolation, without a symbol of saving grace—naked, barren of romance or joy, a thing plucked and polluted by the ruthless hand of necessity.

Then came one of the last stages in the progress of the corn towards the bread-pan of the household. The big, stout ears had to be stripped of the thick outer envelope, and this was called a "corn-husking." It was done by all hands, great and small; the neighbours were invited, the company assembling in the evening, mostly young people; a husking-glove was worn on one hand, and, with a small, knife-shaped implement, the shuck was stripped off and the beautiful gold-red grain was laid bare. This was a time of merry-making, love-making, and gaiety. In the earlier days it was a time of dancing and heavy drinking, but here at the Log-House the evening passed in sober enjoyment, as became the rigid tenets of the master and mistress, almost Calvinistic in their religious views; and so nothing stronger than coffee was drunk at the merry supper which followed.

Six months had passed since the prairie soil was broken for the corn, and now we should see it no more till it came into the house in the form of golden meal, all ready to be prepared for the bread-pan, baked in the oven, and set steaming hot on the table for breakfast or supper, about an inch and a half thick, as yellow as rich gold, the top baked to a brown crust, the whole cut into good-sized squares in the pan. We cut the pieces through the middle and spread them with fresh home-made butter; and this, with home-cured bacon, and eggs laid in the sweet-smelling hay of the old barn, by hens fattened on corn, surpassed any dish I have ever eaten, in the palaces of kings, in the mansions of millionaires, or any of the great restaurants of Paris or London. How many times, when dining with the great ones of the world, undeceived by the illusions of sight, taste, and smell, my mind has wandered back to the delicious breakfasts and suppers at the Log-House, certain that nothing could rival hot corn-bread properly made.

In many of the principal States corn is the staff of life. It is given to pigs, cattle, turkeys, and chickens. It fed the negroes as slaves, the whites when flour was a thing unattainable, gave Abraham Lincoln his robust frame, developed the physical frame of most of the famous men of the South and West of early days, and made victory over malaria and adverse conditions possible. Neurasthenia was unheard-of till the people began to eat bread made from wheat. The eating of hot white biscuits (muffins) for breakfast and supper developed America's national disease—dyspepsia.

Up to the time of the great Civil War, the general type of the South and West was characterised by height, muscular litheness, immense powers of resistance, sound digestion. The fashions in eating kept pace with fashions in dress. Previous to 1820 the dress was mainly of buckskin, cap of fur, such as the raccoon, and moccasins on the feet. Then came the period of jean and linsey-woolsey, dyed blue or copperas-coloured; then what I may call the calico period, when young women were considered to be beautifully dressed in plain dotted or striped coloured calico patterns with sun-bonnets to match. This was followed by a step nearer the city fashions, and ginghams and delaines were introduced here and there; but the silk and lace period did not dawn on the smaller towns of the West till the war suddenly scattered bank-notes broadcast through the land and brought in its train tumult, movement, money, and the latest fashions.

In the autumn there were other gatherings, such as "apple parings," and "quiltings," and the inevitable country fair which everyone attended. The autumn was the most sociable time of the whole year, and for several weeks there would be plenty to do and plenty to talk about. The quilting brought together the most instructive and entertaining visitors. It was a woman's affair, but the husbands usually came for supper at six, or later in the evening, and so there was talk on every subject of any local interest, from politics to mince pies.

After one or two cups of tea Mrs. Busby would talk by the hour, and a word, a hint, would call forth the description of an event or a new version of some disputed story.

"Law me! How this section hez settled up sence we've been here! When we fust come there warn't no stores within a ten-mile ride. It *wuz* rough, and in some places a mite dangerous, especially over in what they called the 'chivaree' district. There wuz a band that chivareed every couple that got married fer miles around; en speakin' o' chivarees reminds me o' the time when ole man Snyder married a yaller-haired gal from down Jerseyville way.

They hedn't more'n got home when 'long come the wust crowd ye could pick up in the hull country, headed by Bub Hawkins en Jack Haywood. They brought ole tin pans, kittles, whistles, cow-bells, horns en everything they could make a howlin' noise with, en set up a kinder war-dance round the cabin. Ole man Snyder was fer shootin', bein' tetchy en not given to lettin' words melt in his mouth, but his bride got riled en took a raw hide en made fer the door, en out she went into the crowd.

" 'Who's the ringleader here?' she says. 'Who's the ringleader? I want te know; en if ye don't tell me I'll cow-hide ye all, en won't be long about it.'

"With that Bub Hawkins started snickerin' en steppin' roun' like a turkey on a hot gridiron, half ashamed like en not knowin' jes' what te do or te say, en Sal Snyder standin' there with her yaller hair all hangin' loose en her eyes a-snappin' like a wild cat.

" 'Ain't ye goin' to tell me?' she shouted; but there warn't a man there that could stand en look right in them eyes.

" 'Looky here, Bub Hawkins,' she says, 'you've come te chivaree me en my ole man, but I'm a-goin' te give ye sumthin' te make ye shiver en keep it up all night,' en with that she lit in en let him have it, head en face, neck en body, en when he broke en ran she wus after him, lettin' him have it from behind; en ye better b'lieve she hed sinews in her arms like the strong man in th' Good Book; en every time Bub Hawkins jumped a log she brought down her cow-hide from behind with a reg'lar war-whoop that made the woods ring. When she had chased the ringleader she come back te tackle the others, but they had all vamosed. They do claim that Sal Snyder plumb broke up that gang.

"They did need religion," she went on, "en it was time Pete Cartwright come along en got Jack Haywood side-tracked from his good-fer-nothin' ways. Ye see, it wus like this: Jack Haywood's wife died en left him with six young uns, en he 'lowed his home wus like a hive without a queen bee. Anyhow, that's what he tole Widder Brown when he married her. Things went 'long purty smooth fer some time, en it looked like he wuz well fixed en settled; but one day she up en said:

" 'Looky here, Jack Haywood, I 'low yer hive's all right, en it sets close te a clover patch; but whar's the honey? I ain't never see ye bring home nothin' but what sticks te yer feet, en thar ain't no mistake 'bout it, thar's plenty comb—fer it's comb, comb, all day long, tryin' te get the hay-seeds out o' yer six sassy tow-heads. Now I tell ye what it is,' she says, turnin' from her dough en p'intin' the rollin'-pin straight at him, 'you've got the hive en you've got a bee te boss it, but what hez *she* got? Why, she's got six young drones, not includin' two yaller dogs en yerself, en if I had wings, ez I hed orter hev, I'd take a bee-line fer a hive that's got some vittles in it.'

"When Uriah asked him how he wus gettin' on with his queen bee, he said:

" 'She's workin' the comb all right, but she stings with her tongue wus'n any hornet I ever bumped agin.'

"His fust wife druv him te drinkin' en this one druv him te religion. He got converted, but fust off she wuz dead set agin preachers, en scuffled up agin preachin' en prayin' in dead earnest till Haywood was most druv crazy. When Pete Cartwright come 'long one day she stormed en raved en used cuss words, en when he said he wuz goin' te pray right in the cabin she shook her fist in his face en 'lowed she wuz one half alligator en t'other half snappin' turtle, en dared him te put her out, ez he said he would if she didn't behave; she said it 'ud take a better man than he wuz te do it.

"While he wuz prayin' she got awful mad. She called him all the names she could think of, en threw the cat at his head, en then Pete Cartwright up en took hold of her arm en swung her clean te the door, en out she went. He slammed the door in her face, en of all the rippin' en roarin' ye ever heared that wuz the wust.

"He barred the door agin her and went right on with his prayin'; but land! with a she-devil scratchin' te get in a man ud hev te be a reg'lar angel with wings not te be riled en flustered in his pleadin's; so he jes' turned the table on her: stopped prayin' en begin to sing ez loud ez ever he could beller—en ye better b'lieve he *could* shout when he got fixed fer it; en the louder she screamed en roared outside, the louder he sung inside, en they kept it up till she begin te pant fer breath. He kept right on till she knocked on the door en hollered out:

" 'Mr. Cartwright, do please let me in!'

" 'Well,' he said, 'I'll let ye come in if ye'll promise te behave yerself.'

"She said she would; so he opened the door en led her te a seat near the fireplace, en he says he never see a woman so pale en tremblin'.

" 'I've been a big fool,' she says.

" 'I 'low ye hev,' says Pete Cartwright, 'en ye'll hev te repent fer all yer sins or ye'll go te perdition.'

"She hung her head en plumb give up fer shame. The poor little children were all huddled under the bed, en he called 'em out en told 'em their mother wouldn't hurt 'em now, en with that he started prayin' agin with Haywood, en in six months she was converted en the folks in that cabin made real happy."

In the evening the riding of the young ladies for prizes at the county fair was discussed. All had something to say concerning this momentous incident.

"I've been attendin' kyounty fairs 'most all my life," said one, "en it did take the rag off the bush te see the way the cuttin's up o' thet ole chestnut sp'iled the ridin' o' them po' gals."

"What I want te know is who put Almedy Sinclair te ride on sech a critter," said another.

"Well," said Mrs. Busby, "ye don't reckon Almedy Sinclair's green enough te pick out sech a rib-breaker te ride on all by herself, do ye?—en she one of the best jedges o' hoss-flesh in this hull deestrict. Why, that gal thinks nothin' o' ridin' bare-back en breakin' the wust mustang ye kin bring her. I've see her do it. She sets a-hossback ez easy ez ye're settin' in that rockin'-cheer. No, sir-ree, ye better look fer someone with more green in their eye before ye ask me te b'lieve she went roamin' roun' the country jes' te choose sech a rip-tearin' bucker fer a saddle-hoss, en she settin' her cap fer fust prize! Almedy Sinclair ain't that kind. Ye see," she continued, warming to the subject, "the man that owned thet chestnut fust off went te the Mexican War en rid him in the battle o'

Bueny Visty, en there's where a bullet nipped the top off one o' his marrer-bones, a leetle behind the saddle, en that wuz the beginnin' o' the kickin' en the buckin'; but some say after the wowned got healed he kept the buckin' up jest fer old times' sake. When his owner come back from the war he sold him fer a good draw-hoss, b'lievin' him te be right safe te pull a wagon, en when the man that bought him was fordin' a creek in flood-time the hoss kicked everything te pieces right in the middle o' the creek. His next owner was a Baptist preacher who took te dram drinkin' te drown his sorrer at bein' so tuck in by a sleek, fat hoss en a professin' Christian. The fac' is, the wowned in his back got healed quick enough, en it never showed no signs on th' outside, but the bone wuz allers tender, en when the saddle wus put a leetle too fur back, er when it happened te be a leetle too long, there was sure to be trouble; en that double-dealin' rascal that owns him now knows it, en he fixed te hev Almedy lose en his own gal win, fer he knew if Almedy hed a good hoss she'd surely carry off the prize.

"Ye see, when a body's used te ridin' hosses that chaw the bit en prance te one side en rear on their hind legs, it looks like hoss en gal's both cunnin' 'nough te show off their good p'ints all te oncet, en Almedy Sinclair kinder looked fer sumthin' like that in the critter she was ridin'. She expected te be h'isted a couple o' times, fer a man hollered out to her, 'Sit ez tight ez ye kin!' en she knowed what that meant; but it didn't mean what she thought. Th' old chestnut warn't no ways stiff in the hind legs when he started; but that ain't allers a good sign nuther. It allers takes time te git right down te the weak spot of any beast, but in this here case it looked like the time wus fore-ordained, ez the preachers say, right down te the minnit, fer jest ez th' ole hoss come along in front o' the jedges' stand the saddle worked back till it come agin the tender marrer-bone, en he stopped like he'd been struck with a bullet. Right then I hear a man say, 'Watch out!' en skasely hed he spoke when the critter up en give his tail en hind legs sech a twist that it looked like Almedy'd surely land on the critter's neck. It warn't expected; the hoss riz at the wrong end. There he stood, stock still, leavin' Almedy Sinclair settin' like a sack o' seed pertaters while t'other gal rid by on her prancin' roan ez big ez life en twicet ez sassy. Pore Almedy sot till her hoss riz en shuck his heels agin, en ye kin b'lieve she made a break from that saddle ez mad ez ever ye see a gal in all yer born days."

Chapter XI

The Flight

THE Indian summer had come, the season of seasons, with its golden memories, its diaphanous skies, its dream-like afternoons, its gossamer veils spread over the shimmering horizon, transforming by its own transcendent magic the whole earth and atmosphere.

Smoke rose from wooded places in long, thin columns of hazy blue, and once in a while a whiff of burning grass and leaves filled the magnetic air with fragrant odour. The settlers ceased to fret and worry; there was neither reaping nor repining.

The sun was setting when I arrived at the Load-Bearer's home, two days after Isaac Snedeker's visit to the Log-House. I had brought more provisions for the fugitives.

"Dear me! but yer ma *is* good te send all these vittles fer the runaways," exclaimed Mrs. Gest as I emptied my saddle-bags on the kitchen table.

As I was going to stay there till morning we sat about here and there waiting for the hours to pass and the coming of Isaac Snedeker, who was to take the fugitives to the next station that night. We expected his arrival some time between ten and eleven o'clock.

How calm and peaceful was the evening!

Now and then a gentle current of wind stirred the branches, and the leaves fell in flaky showers like snow on ground already strewn with the dead foliage of autumn.

Far away, the tinkling of bells told of cattle peacefully grazing, and the prairie, immense and tranquil as a golden sea, inspired a feeling as of ages and ages of repose.

In the west a bank of filmy clouds edged with silver floated against a sky of glassy green which gradually melted into serried ranks of flaming amber, and the sere, crisp leaves of the beech were interlaced with the red and purple of oak and maple, while the trees by the creek glistened and sparkled in the genial rays of the setting sun.

And there was something in the early hours of the evening that throbbed in ceaseless unison with the constellations overhead. After darkness closed in all the witchery of Nature seemed at work in earth and sky. Above the tree-tops a host of twinkling stars looked down on the anxious watchers and refugees. Presently a thin mist descended about us through which the starry vault and dark masses of trees could be discerned, with tracings of dim, fantastic forms in the scattered underbush.

The slanting rays of the rising moon came reaching in long gleams across the roof of the little frame house, while its weird shafts shot through the narrow interspaces of wood and thicket, and gleamed in small round patches on the green moss underneath. The scarlet vines all around on the boughs were tipped with a soft, glistening pallor that fell as from some ghostly lantern from a distant world, while just above the horizon, poised like an aerial plume in the deep indigo blue, the vanishing comet waned amidst a wilderness of glittering lights under a shimmering crown of stars.

During a moment of profound quiet, when it seemed as if all Nature had sunk to rest, a wolf beyond the creek began a series of long-drawn-out howls. The woods began to vibrate with low, clamorous calls. The howling drew nearer; one of the wolf-hounds answered back in pitiful cries, then another and another. Everywhere call answered call. A rushing sound filled the space above us where vast flocks of wildfowl cut the air with the swish and rustle of a thousand wings. The honking came and went as flock after flock passed over us in whizzing waves. The whole world was stirring. Earth sent up a chorus of lamentations that mingled with the voices above. The fugitives huddled together in the cave in expectation of some unimagined calamity, and at last, unable to withstand the feeling of terror, they began to creep up towards the house.

The Load-Bearer, who had gone into the kitchen, fell on his knees, with the Bible open before him on the chair, while his wife sat just inside, with her hands tightly clasped, peering intently through the open door across the clear patches of moonlight.

Soon he rose and hurriedly walked out.

"Whar be ye goin'?" stammered his wife, noticing his dazed look.

He walked as one in a dream, while Cornelia followed.

"Elihu, whar be ye goin'?"

There was a clinking of the chains at the kennels, and a cry from the wolf-hounds told us they were free. They sped round and round the house in a whirl of excitement, then into the woods and back again to the house, giving the last shudder to the climax of confusion before they made off towards the main road leading south-west.

Then, as by a wave of some invisible wand, the tumult ceased. The woods and the house lay plunged in an all-pervading stillness. The country round about seemed suddenly dipped in a gulf of silence.

The Load-Bearer came back to the kitchen and again fell on his knees. After some moments he began to read aloud:

" 'Alas, for that day is great, so that none is like it; it is even the time of Jacob's trouble; but he shall be saved out of it.' "

"Whar be they?" mused Cornelia, not listening to her husband. "It's gettin' late . . . Brother Snedeker said he'd be here at ten o'clock."

Her hair had fallen down on one side of her face; she looked sad and very troubled. She was overburdened with the loads of others, with loads which she had not sought, which life and death had heaped together in one short, swift period of time, and she felt crushed under their weight. But Elihu Gest, absorbed in prayer, heard nothing, saw nothing, thought of nothing but the Eternal.

Now he read aloud from Isaiah:

" 'Awake, awake, O Jerusalem, which hast drunk of the hand of the Lord the cup of His fury; thou hast drunken the dregs of the cup of trembling and wrung them out.' "

He remained silent for a moment, and when he continued it was with a voice full of prophetic faith:

" 'Thus saith the Lord thy God that pleadeth the cause of His people, behold I have taken out of thine hand the cup of trembling, even the dregs of the cup of My fury; thou shalt no more drink it again.' "

The last words had sunk deep into Cornelia's soul. She seemed to have caught all the mystical power of those seven magical words: "Thou shalt no more drink it again." Her eyes grew brighter, her face was lit by a placid smile, all the old religious faith came rushing back.

A faint breeze brought with it an aroma of dried leaves and withering grasses. As the moon rose higher in the heavens the night grew brighter. Not far from the door a group of fugitives stood gazing intently at Cornelia Gest, the pallid faces of the octoroons forming a sort of spectral frame for the black faces in the centre. Here and there, around the house, murmurs and half-suppressed groans and supplications arose, for the runaways had brought to the Load-Bearer's home a new world, with new and unheard-of influences. There were fugitives from nearly every slave State bordering the Mississippi; they brought with them their own peculiar beliefs, their own interpretations of certain signs and sounds of the night. All had been awed by the appearance of the comet, but now a terrible fear possessed them. For each one every sound came as a special menace, every object had a special symbol.

The Load-Bearer rose from his knees, and as he stepped to the door one of the wolf-hounds, covered with bloodstains, was there to greet him. The others were not far off, and all had evidently done their work.

"Somethin' hez happened down on the road," said Cornelia.

"They hev nipped some evil in the bud," returned Elihu.

But Cornelia peered without ceasing in one direction, anxiously awaiting the arrival of Isaac Snedeker.

"Thar's someone a-comin' now," remarked the Load-Bearer.

But we still waited, gazing into the distance. The last hour had seemed endless. We walked down towards the creek to pass away the time, then returned and stood in the moonlight. Elihu Gest was trying to make out what the object was that we now saw approaching from the east. It came looming up in the thin mist that hung over the road, growing bigger as it drew nearer; and the fugitives, seeing it approach, sought refuge in the darkness behind the house, some running as far as the creek.

Not one was visible; not a murmur was to be heard. A ghostly silence greeted Azariah James, the preacher, as he came ambling up on a horse that seemed to glide over the surface of the ground. There he sat for some moments, speechless, and at first I did not recognise him, clad as he was in hunting costume, with a fringe about the cape, a coon-skin cap on his head, a rifle slung over his shoulders, and a pistol and dirk before him.

But the man himself had not changed. It was the same face, naïvely absent-minded and wonderingly mute, that I had seen at the meeting-house—the man who began his sermon by a series of blunders and then glided along by some miraculous means to an unexpected and memorable triumph. Now, as then, he looked as if he were floating along with the tide and the hour, ready for the unforeseen without expecting it, armed for trouble without fearing it.

We stood looking at the preacher and he at us, but no one spoke.

What an enigmatical group we must have been to the peeping fugitives a little distance away! There sat Azariah James, the preacher, twin brother in spirit to Elihu Gest, the Load-Bearer; yet what a contrast they presented! The preacher appeared double his natural size, clothed in a hunter's garb, awaiting some mysterious command; and the Load-Bearer, thinner, smaller, almost wizened, seemed to be awaiting some word or sign on the part of the preacher.

And a sign did come; but not from Azariah James. Down to the south, through the thick groves of beech, a yellow light rose and fell and rose again in slow waving flashes over the horizon, its glow reaching above the wooded cover, and even beyond the belted line of timber to the east.

"What kin thet be?"

It was Cornelia who spoke, for the two men were still rapt in a kind of mystical quandary.

"Thar's sunthin' goin' on down thar er my name ain't Elihu Gest, en the Lord ain't sent ye, Azariah," remarked the Load-Bearer.

"I 'low ye're right," replied the preacher; "the prairie's a-burnin' cl'ar from a mile beyon' Lem Stephens's, plumb te the bend in the creek."

"The prairie on fire, en at this time o' night!" exclaimed Cornelia; "what kin it mean?"

"Why, it means that the Almighty air with we uns, en agin Lem Stephens en the slave-catchers."

"Air it runnin' him clost?"

"Ez fur ez I kin jedge it must be closin' in on him about now," responded the preacher, with surprising nonchalance. "A passel o' good-fer-nothin's banded tharselves together te come over en take off the runaways en git the rewards. They 'lowed te be hyar by this time so ez te head off Brother Snedeker. I come right by Lem Stephens's en see 'em let the bloodhounds loose, en jest ez the hounds lit out over this way the prairie began te blaze, so all hands stayed right thar te watch the place."

The Load-Bearer began to shake off his seeming lethargy.

"Whar be the bloodhounds now?" he asked.

"Whar be they? I reckon they air right whar yer dogs en my pistol left 'em down the road thar."

"They air dead!" cried Cornelia.

"Dey air dead!" echoed a mournful voice behind the house.

The cry was taken up by other fugitives, who imagined Isaac Snedeker and his friends had been assassinated.

"Dey's all dead! Dey done killed 'em off!" arose on all sides from the dark forms now emerging from their hiding-places.

An ever-increasing glamour shone through the woods to the south, and the runaways now saw it for the first time. It hushed their cries and murmurs as if a damper had suddenly been placed over their mouths.

Azariah James got off his horse, tied up, and followed Cornelia Gest into the kitchen.

" 'Pears like they won't never git here to-night," she sighed.

" 'Bout how many d'ye expect?"

"Brother Snedeker en two er three more; but he's a-comin' te carry the runaways te the nex' station. I don't calc'late he'll stay more'n long 'nough te load up en git away ez quick ez iver he kin."

There were sounds of horses' hoofs and wagon wheels outside.

Cornelia Gest went to the door.

"Thank the Lord ye've got here at last!" she exclaimed, greeting a slender man with a long, greyish beard, who was helping out an elderly woman clad in deep black.

"It's Squar Higgins," said Cornelia; "en Sister Higgins hez come along te cher a body by thet beautiful smile o' her'n; Elihu allers says it's like the grace o' God a-smilin' on the hull world when *she's* aroun'."

And so it was; for Martha Higgins was another of those wonderful women whose very presence diffused an influence of peace and harmony. Her faith and confidence in the Divine goodness were incorruptible and never-ending. She brought with her a radiant power that aroused the preacher to thoughts of praise and thanksgiving for all the mercies of the past and present. With her presence, the terrors of the night receded, and the preacher, with his eyes half closed, began to hum a few bars of a favourite hymn.

Meanwhile the Load-Bearer had quietly slipped away

to have a look over the prairie. He had climbed a large withered tree which stood on a knoll, and was watching a thin tongue of fire licking up the grass away towards the bend in the creek not far from Lem Stephens's frame house. From this tree he had often looked out before, but never on such a sight as this. He watched the flames dart up here and there in sudden flashes as they caught the strips of taller grass in the low soil near the water, dying down where the ground was higher and the grass thinner. He could not at first make out in what direction the flames were moving, nor could he yet tell whether they had reached the frame house. The whole region before him lay circled in a rim of fire. Never had he been in such intimate communion with the mighty forces of the Eternal; never had he felt the breath of the night come with so much inspiration. It seemed to Elihu Gest that fire had descended from the skies, that a ban had been placed on the movements of evil-doers in that section and for miles around; and while he pondered and marvelled over the wonders of the night he felt the "Living Presence" throb through his being with a quickening power that lifted him clear above and away from mortal things. He shouted aloud one of his favourite passages from the Old Testament. He was about to descend when a long sheet of flame leaped into the sky. Lem Stephens's house was ablaze: it was burning like a box of tinder. Now the barn caught; now the brushwood behind the house was blazing. The border of the creek was a mass of flame. It looked as if a fiery serpent were moving in a zigzag along its border, rising and falling on great wings of fire, then disappearing, to rise again in another place.

A current of wind was created by the heat, and flames darted from the other side of the water.

When he returned, Elihu Gest found Isaac Snedeker —who had brought several more refugees with him—the two Higginses, Azariah James, and Cornelia, all sitting in a semi-circle in the kitchen, and after greeting Mr. Snedeker he took a seat at one end.

There followed a period of deep, devotional quietude in which each one sat as if alone. There was the grey-bearded Squire Higgins, with his big brows and kindly face; there was Cornelia Gest, slender, frail, and shrunken, in her seat; there was Azariah James, whose broodings defied all divination; there was Isaac Snedeker, stern and restless as an eagle about to take wing; and Martha Higgins, whose high, massive forehead and arching nose contrasted strangely with the bountiful kindness of her dreamy eyes, while her smile expressed a faith that was infinite and undying.

At one end sat Elihu Gest, obscure carrier of other people's loads, impulsive and enigmatical seer, last in the long procession of the *ante-bellum* prophets of old Illinois.

A shout was heard, and Elihu looked at Martha Higgins as he said:

"They ain't calc'lated te understand what it air thet's workin' out te save them."

"Martha had a presentiment before we came," observed Squire Higgins. "I have never known her to be wrong."

"Who lit thet fire?" queried Cornelia Gest. " 'Twarn't you, Brother Snedeker?"

"That's what I've been wanting to know. I came near

being caught in it, and now I'll have to wait here till I see how far it's going to spread."

"It hez plumb licked up Lem Stephens's house," said the Load-Bearer. "I see it from the big tree."

"I want te know!" exclaimed Cornelia.

"Thar ain't nothin' left by this time. If Lem Stephens en the slave-hunters ain't hidin' in the water they air burnt up. Thar's a mighty power movin' over the yearth; I ain't see a night sech ez this sence the comet fust appeared."

Isaac Snedeker went out with Squire Higgins to survey the land. A wall of fire rose above the creek, to the south; an immense, palpitating glow lit the sky—a glow that flashed like sheet-lightning along the course of the creek, for a wind had risen which forced the flames straight towards the Load-Bearer's home. There was a rushing sound where it began to skim the upper branches; then a current of warm air struck through the open space leading from the creek to the house. The woods rang with the screaming of birds; the howling of a wolf again haunted the lonely plains to the north, and a little later an awful roar told that the fire had reached the tall, thick grass and brushwood that lined the water's edge not more than a quarter of a mile from the house.

"De comet done struck de yearth! De world's burnin' up!"

The runaways no longer thought of slave-hunters and a return to bondage. For them, all was at an end; and from a sort of dumb despair there issued forth groans and exclamations of, "Mercy, Lord, mercy, mercy!"

Yet two or three were on the point of escaping to the woods.

Isaac Snedeker, seeing the danger, called out:

"All who run away will be caught!"

Squire Higgins hardly knew what to do. The night seemed like day. The roar of the fire could be heard, ever a little nearer, ever more ominous and awful.

"If we have to quit," he said at last, "there's not a minute to lose!"

He was thinking of the safety of the women.

Even the invincible Isaac Snedeker was shaken by forebodings of evil. But when they returned to the kitchen and beheld the Load-Bearer in the same place, self-poised, self-contained, all doubts departed.

" 'Twixt here and thar, thar's a swamp and a patchin' o' oak thet won't ketch, en the grass air sparse and spindlin', en then comes the big trees. But thar's sunthin' else besides the wind thet's blowin' them flames, Squar Higgins."

Even as he spoke the light from the fire was gradually descending out of the zenith. Lower and lower it fell. In about ten minutes nothing but a dim outline of glimmering yellow could be discerned far beyond the belt of woods, and once more the moonlight reigned; the patches of light were brighter, the shadows deeper; the wings of unrest were folded, and silence returned with a twofold presage.

"It air about time," said the Load-Bearer, rising and placing his hand on the preacher's shoulder. "It air time te begin," he intimated to Squire Higgins and Isaac Snedeker.

They all left the kitchen except Cornelia Gest, Martha Higgins, and myself. Cornelia's face assumed a pensive look; she wiped away a tear, and said in a quavering voice:

"God be praised! He allowed her te pass out o' this world in peace. I'm right happy te have ye here, Sister Higgins, en I jes' knowed ye'd come over when Elihu sent ye word."

"I don't know of anything that could have kept me from coming, Sister Gest," replied Mrs. Higgins. "I had a presentiment that she would die right here."

"We couldn't git her te talk about herself, nur give her name, nur nothin'; they're all so afeared they'll be sent back te bondage. Thar ain't on'y Mr. Snedeker en Brother James en yerselves ez knows 'bout her havin' died here. If thar warn't so many good people aroun' I'd give right up, seein' so many wicked. But Elihu said he war boun' te have prayers en his favourite hymn sung at the funeral."

Now for the first time I knew that the quadroon had passed away and that this night was appointed for her burial.

We had not long to wait, for presently Squire Higgins came and announced that all was ready. When we got to the graveside, near the creek, all the fugitives stood around, some of them holding lanterns, the black faces appearing strangely unnatural in the flickering light, the faces of the quadroons and octoroons more ghostly. Under the trees, half in the moonlight, half in shadow, it seemed as if a great multitude were crowding up from behind, eager to catch every sound that might pass from anyone's lips.

A soft breeze moved among the last sere leaves of autumn. Now and then a gentle gust swayed the lower branches to and fro, and an infinitely tender sighing came and went and melted away in the eerie moonlight.

The preacher took off his tightly-fitting cap and without it his hair stood out in wild, rumpled locks. He seemed to loom taller and taller. He looked as if he had forgotten all he had intended to say, and was standing there helpless and forsaken at the brink of a grave, over the dead he had come to bury.

"Praise God!" murmured the Load-Bearer, who alone of all the persons there seemed to understand.

Azariah James closed his eyes for one or two seconds; a slight shiver passed through his frame; then he opened them wide and searching, and a wondrous light flashed out over the awed and speechless company. He was no longer an awkward, hesitating dreamer, but a lion aroused, a prophet in his own country. His listeners began to move and sway in unison with his immeasurable compassion, and after he had spoken for ten minutes the Load-Bearer offered up a short, fervent prayer. Then, when the last scene was about to begin, the voice of Martha Higgins rang out above the open grave:

> "On Jordan's stormy banks I stand
> And cast a wistful eye"—

A loud, rolling wave of song passed in long, reaching echoes through the woods as the twenty-nine persons present sent their voices calling—

"To Canaan's fair and happy land
  Where my possessions lie"—

for now every voice was attuned to the old matchless melody of the meeting-house and the camp ground.

As the hymn proceeded the sense of time was obliterated. A far-sweeping chorus, tinged here and there with a nameless melancholy, floated upward into the white silence of the night. On and on they sang, and the old hymn rolled out in a miracle of sound, on a river of golden melody, vibrating far into regions of infinite light and love.

Isaac Snedeker gathered up the runaways and prepared for flight. He separated them into two groups—one he would carry in his own wagon, the other was for Squire Higgins. It did not take long, and the two wagon loads set out in the clear moonlight. A little way towards the north they would separate, each going according to a pre-arranged plan; and every fugitive arrived at last safely in Canada, which was, after all, the land of Canaan for them.

Chapter XII

The Camp-Meeting

ON THE morning of the great camp-meeting I stood at the gate for nearly an hour waiting for a sight of the Busby wagon, which was to take us; and when it arrived Uriah Busby was so eager to be off that his wife had barely time to call out to those standing at the door to see us depart:

"You see it's jest as I said, Uriah says he'll git there if it was twice as fur agin."

When we got to the main road we began to see signs of gathering campers, but when we reached a place called the "mud-holes" people could be seen in every direction making for this spot where several roads converged into one.

"Now, Uriah, you ain't a-goin' to land us in the mud, air ye?" said Mrs. Busby, as we neared the deceitful holes. "If there ain't them Wagner boys, plague take 'em! I do hope we kin git through afore they do."

"I reckon they ain't been drinking yet," said her husband; "it's too early in the day."

"I don't know 'bout that," returned Serena Busby. "They don't look accommodatin', en ye see they're doin' their level best to git ahead of us."

The Wagner boys were urging on their horses almost to a gallop.

"Now, Uriah, don't be a fool; jest rein up en let 'em go it all they want to; the folks at the camp ain't a-goin' to shout much afore we git there; en besides, if ye dump me in the mud it'll be the fust en the last time."

Uriah Busby did as he was told. The Wagner boys made a dash for the crossing, but in the rush to be first they went too far to the right. When they got to the middle, at a place where the mud looked shallow but was in reality deep, over went the wagon and out toppled the brothers.

"Providence air on our side," said Uriah, as he took extra pains to keep to the left.

"It'll take some o' the dare-devil out of 'em, en if it had been a Baptist camp-meetin' it 'ud took some sousin' in the creek to wash the mud from their bodies as well as the sins from their souls," remarked Mrs. Busby.

Other travellers followed, all giving that particular side of the crossing a wide berth. In about three hours we arrived at another point where we could see scores of people in wagons, buggies, and on horseback, making for the camp, now distant about an hour. Many of the horses "carried double," while in some of the big covered wagons sat whole families. A blinding dust filled the air and covered our clothes, as we drove along in the wake of others, receiving their dust and kicking more of it up for those at our heels. As the day began to grow hot we saw many indulging in "drams" from the demijohn, and Serena Busby remarked that there was sure to be some "kickin'-up" at the camp towards evening.

As we got within two miles of the grounds the whole
populace, for a radius of many miles, seemed to be on the
move, converging towards one point. From a slight
eminence which we had just attained, commanding a view
on all sides, a scraggy line of white-topped wagons could
be seen descending a slope to the right, while to the left,
a little below us, another line of twisting vehicles ascended
in a slow, weary train, enveloped in clouds of dust, now
partly hidden behind clumps of trees, now emerging like
the remnant of some scattered army crawling towards the
precincts of a friendly country. Once in a while we were
passed by young men on horseback who galloped their
horses; others, in light buggies, shot past the heavy
wagons and were soon out of sight; hundreds were on
foot, looking neither to the right nor to the left, and
these, as Uriah Busby observed, were the ones in dead
earnest, bound to get there no matter how.

We drove into the camp grounds about one o'clock,
and found two or three thousand persons already there,
with others pouring in by the hundred.

A shed had been erected large enough to shelter several
thousand persons, and out in the woods, beyond the con-
fines of the meeting-grounds, groups of old reprobates and
young rowdies had taken their stand with whisky barrels
and demijohns ready to supply all who cared for strong
drink, some of them armed with pistols and murderous-
looking knives. Everyone was eating or getting ready to
eat, for the women had brought a goodly supply of edi-
bles. Tents were put up by some, while others would sleep
in the covered wagons, the men mostly under the wagons
or under the shed. It looked like an immense gathering

for a picnic; and it was impossible to say from the expression of people's faces what sort of a meeting it was, for no one seemed over-anxious; all seemed contented to be there let come what may. Indeed, Mrs. Busby was right when she said:

"Te jedge by thar looks they hev all saved their souls en air now attendin' to thar bodies, not te git te the other world afore thar time."

Uriah Busby unhitched the horses at a spot near the creek, and after dinner Serena began to look about her.

Presently she discovered someone she knew.

"Why, if thar ain't Zack Caverly, of all people in the world!"

"Wal, I'll be blamed!" exclaimed Mr. Busby. "Ye don't reckon he's come te sell whisky, do ye?"

"I reckon not. Zack's ez sober ez an owl, en ye know it. Wal! If there ain't Minerva Wagner! I want to know how she got here! Must hev come a-hossback, if she didn't come in a neighbour's wagon, fearin' to risk her neck with them two good-fer-nothin's."

And, sure enough, there was Mrs. Wagner, seated on a big stump, talking to Ebenezer Hicks.

"My word!" said Uriah Busby; "it do give me a disagreeable feelin' te see them fire-eatin' Baptists settin' there waitin' fer te stir up mischief agin the Abolitionists en the Methodists. They ain't out here fer any good, I kin tell ye."

"You better b'lieve they ain't here fer any religion they kin pick up; I believe I ain't never seen her look so sour and spiteful."

Zack Caverly led his horse over and settled himself near our wagon.

"I heared ye war comin'," he said, "en the weather bein' fine I fixed te ride over en take things sort o' easy durin' meetin'-time."

"Hev ye see many folks ye know?" asked Uriah Busby.

"The whole kintry's turnin' out; thar's goin' te be the biggest meetin' ever holdin' in this section. Ye see, it's the fire-eatin' question thet's got hold on 'em, en they all want te see which a-way the black cat's a-goin' te jump. Summow, right er wrong, the people hev an idee that this here meetin' ain't so much fer religion ez it air fer politics, en thet's why ye see so many Baptists en Campbellites en Presbyterians en members o' the Methodist Church South sprinkled all over the grounds. I heared a man say they've got Abe Lincoln on the brain."

" 'Pears to me," said Mrs. Busby, "it's niggers more likely."

The afternoon and evening of Thursday were given up to preliminary services and to getting the huge meeting into working order, and on Friday afternoon the number of people on the ground was computed at twenty thousand.

Religious services were held three times a day, and in case of a revival the evening service would be protracted far into the night, perhaps all night, as it often happened at such gatherings. But somehow the meetings on Friday seemed without any signs of enthusiasm; the people listened with respect to all that was said, and they sang with a hearty will, but there was something lacking. Uriah

Busby remarked to Zack Caverly that it was a spark from Heaven that was wanting, to which the old pioneer replied that he thought so too, as there was plenty of tinder in the congregation.

Before the evening service on this day, Friday, Elihu Gest, Squire Higgins, Azariah James, and several others decided on going out into the woods to a lonely spot and praying for a revival at the next service.

The people were all expectation at meeting-time, the preachers did their best, exhorters exhorted, but there were no happy shouts, no groans of mental misery, no conviction of sins. Squire Higgins said he had often seen the like before, and counselled hope and courage, but the Load-Bearer was certain they had not prayed with sufficient faith and fervour. "The people," he declared, "air all right, but they must be tetched."

Saturday came, and at the morning service it was decided to have a short but positive sermon on the sins of the times, with some pointed remarks against slavery; for a good many were of the opinion that this would fire up the people and prepare a way for a revival in the afternoon. The sermon was preached by a stranger from Missouri, but it failed to do more than create a lively interest in the political questions of the hour, and, curious to relate, just as this meeting was brought to a close the negroes on the ground, who numbered between two and three hundred, began a meeting of their own off at one side of the white camp, where certain freed negroes were found who actually believed in slavery.

Their meeting was conducted in the orthodox Methodist manner; but those of the coloured people who belonged to the Methodist Church South were believers in slavery, while the Methodist Church North was against it, many of its members being extreme Abolitionists. The coloured meeting was conducted by two negro exhorters, presided over by a white preacher, and when the exercises began by the singing of a popular hymn:

> "De golden chariot's hangin' low,
> My breddern you'll be called on"—

the whole meeting, as Zack Caverly said, was soon put in the "weaving way"; the great yellow eyes began to roll in a sort of subdued ecstasy, the black faces beamed contentment, and woolly heads rocked in keeping with the lilt of the music.

It was not long before a tall, glossy black negro, with small, piercing eyes and thick lips, rose, and with a look of mingled humour and cynicism, began to speak.

"Breddern an' sistern," he said; "some o' you done hearn w'at de preacher ober in de white camp said 'bout dis yer slavery biznuz, an' I wuz askin' to myself ez I sot an' heared you all singin' an' gettin' happy—which is better fer de coloured folks, to be boun' in dis wurrul an' free in de nex', er te be free in dis wurrul an' boun' after you am dead?"

He licked his lips and eyed the congregation for a moment before proceeding.

"I ain't got time to stan' heah an' answer no questions 'bout de rights an' de wrongs ob de coloured folks, but I 'low dar's some folks in dis meetin' wat's run away fr'm der mastahs an' ain't in no hurry to go back. But which am it better to do—cross ober Jordan inter Canaan, er cross de State line inter Canada? I's gwine to make de observation 'bout de black snake w'at change his skin, kase some ob you settin' heah to-day done gone and made de change an' ain't noways better off.

"Dar wuz a black snake w'at lef' home an' 'gin ter wander roun', but de sun gittin' sorter hot he say ter hissef, 'I reckin hit's 'bout time fer to shed dis heah skin, hit gittin' too hot to carry'; so he des slip hit off, an' he done felt he gwine ter fly instead er crawl on de groun'. When de night come on de wedder done git mighty cole, an' 'fo' long he come 'cross a skin a rattlesnake des shuck hissef out'n. Mist' black snake say ter hissef, 'I des 'bout slip in dar an' keep warm'; but he ain't no sooner slip in dan 'long come a white man wid a big stick an' he say, 'I don't nebber kill no black snakes, but I kill all de rattle-snakes I ebber come 'cross,' and wid dat he up an' kill de black snake fust lick.

"Now, breddern, dis heah ain't no sermon. I'se speakin' in w'at dey calls de paraboils; dat's de meanin' ob de observation fer de coloured folks, an' dat is—don't nebber change yo' 'ligion, an' don't nebber run away fr'm yo' masters."

Despair took possession of the runaways who were sitting listening, and during the proceedings that followed one of the fugitives sought counsel of Isaac Snedeker, who was attending the camp-meeting and who had arranged that a number of runaways were to gather here, this being considered the safest plan that could be devised to accomplish their liberation. The sensation created by the negro's story was such that for the space of half an hour no preaching, nor singing, nor exhorting would move the congregation; but after a vigorous effort on the part of the preacher and exhorters a movement of revival became apparent at the farthest end of the meeting, seeing which one of the exhorters pointed over the heads of the people, and, with an angry look, cried out:

"Muster up dem mo'ners dar! Prone 'em up, Brudder Dixon. Brudder Luke Henry, mourn up dem w'ats a-pantin' an' faintin' down dar in de furder aisle. Sis' Jones, whar's yo' singin'-voice? You ain't been out las' night a-imitatin' dem squinch-owls, is you? Now, help 'long dar! I 'low we goin' keep Satan fr'm clippin' yo' wings by de Lord's help dis day."

The meeting of the coloured people proceeded in due order, and by the time it came to an end the afternoon service began in the main camp. The people sat and listened but did not respond, and some of the leaders were haunted by a presentiment of failure. To make matters worse, the drunken rowdies beyond the camp began to harass the preachers from the rear, near the creek. Under the influence of cheap, fiery whisky some of them acted like madmen, and a plan was concocted to duck Azariah James in the creek in the evening, after the last service.

The evening meeting began early and lasted till late. At its close another consultation was held among the preachers. Once more it was declared necessary to go out and plead for grace and power to bring about a revival. Uriah Busby advised his wife to invite Elihu Gest and Azariah James over to the wagon to take a "cold check, ez brother Gest looks clean washed out en Brother James caved in, after that long sermon o' his'n."

"A cold check!" exclaimed Serena; "you better b'lieve

they want sumthin' else besides hard boiled eggs en bread en butter. I'll fix 'em up some real strong coffee, steamin' hot. I kin boil the water in a jiffy in that new kittle we brought 'long; en I calc'late *we'll* take a nip o' sumthin' er nuther ez long ez we're 'bout it, fer I feel a mite caved in myself, en I reckon ye all do. I declare to goodness, Uriah, I ain't see ye look so floppy sence the comet scare!"

The two invited guests came, and Mrs. Busby spread a cloth on the ground and was about to prepare the meal with the hot coffee when suddenly the Load-Bearer interposed:

"Jes' wait a while, Sister Busby. 'Tain't no use—I cain't wrastle with the sperrit on a full stommick. I ain't never hed no prayers answered that a-way. We've got te go out yander en pray, en if ever I felt the need of it, it's right now."

"The meetin' wus sorter cold, en thet's a fac'," said Uriah Busby.

"It war lukewarm; thet's the wust thing a man kin say, for it shows thet the people feel comfortable-like in thar sins."

"It's a pity Pete Cartwright's too feeble to be here," remarked Serena, "fer if he wuz he'd put 'em into hot water quicker'n lightnin'. A lot o' them folks don't want preachin' half so much ez brimstone; some preachers carry it in their pockets like, en jes' throw it over the people."

The preachers were gone about a quarter of an hour and then returned to the Busby wagon and partook of refreshments. The Load-Bearer's face was beaming with contentment.

"I feel like our prayers hev been heared at the throne o' grace," he said, as he seated himself on the ground and took the coffee Mrs. Busby offered him in a large tin cup; "en this is the fust time I've hed the feelin' since the meetin' opened. Te-morrer's the day."

"It most allers is," remarked Uriah.

"Thet's so," added Mrs. Busby; "it takes two or three days fer a meetin' like this te git het through en through."

"I hev noticed more'n oncet how Sunday kin be favoured by an outpourin' o' the Sperrit; en if Sunday passes 'thout a shakin' o' dry bones thar ain't much hope left fer any protracted meetin'."

"Thet's a fac', Brother Gest," remarked Azariah James; "Sunday's the holy day in more ways 'n one. What's done hez te be done, en will be done te-morrer."

"Here comes Brother Snedeker!"

"Law me!" exclaimed Serena. "I've been wonderin' what hed become o' ye."

"And I have been hunting for you all," he said, coming up to the circle. "There are a good many rowdies and cut-throats on the outskirts of the camp, and it looks as if they were hatching mischief; they have been drinking hard all the evening and are still at it."

"Air thar any slave-drivers among 'em?" asked Uriah.

"Not that I know of, but they are all enemies of this meeting, and they are being encouraged by the whisky-drinkers and pro-slavery Christians."

"But we ain't been disturbed in the meetin's yet, that's one good thing."

"No, but there's been fighting out round the whisky-wagons every time the people assemble for preaching. We are forming a company to protect the preachers and the services to-morrow. We've got to get at least a hundred men enrolled as watchmen, and another hundred who will swear to up and help if the watchmen prove insufficient."

"I ain't got no special fears noways," said Elihu Gest; "that is, not now."

"But ye hed before ye went out te wrastle," said Uriah Busby.

"I tell you what it is, brethren," said Isaac Snedeker, "I shall not be able to remain at the camp longer than to-morrow midnight. I have three or four loads of runaways to look after, and you, Brother Gest, will have to take a party of ten. Brother James will be allotted about the same number, and I'll take as many as my wagon will hold."

"I reckon," said the Load-Bearer, "we'll hev te fix te git cl'ar o' the camp by Sunday night, fust thing arter preachin' closes."

"Here comes Squire Higgins!" exclaimed Serena; "sumthin's th' matter!"

"We want all hands over by the preachers' tent," he said hurriedly; "there's going to be trouble."

The Squire carried a stout hickory stick, and advised all the others to arm themselves with the same kind of weapon.

Most of the campers were asleep by this time, but as we approached the spot indicated excited talk could be heard and groups of men gathered as if in consultation.

The preachers' tent stood behind the public platform, midway between it and the creek, and here stood the wagons, buggies, and rockaways of the preachers and elders. The ruffians began by imitating the crowing of cocks, the squealing of pigs, the shouting of "convicted" sinners, the mewing of cats; and while one band was engaged in holding the attention of the preachers, another began to move off one of the buggies to roll it over the bank into the creek, which was ten feet deep at this place.

Elder Johnson's buggy was already wheeled to within a few feet of the bank; two of the rowdies were about to let it fall into the water when Isaac Snedeker brought his hickory stick down on the back of the leader with such force that a cry of pain went up from the culprit. The buggy was abandoned, but, in the meantime, Azariah James had been seized from behind by two powerful ruffians and was being led to the creek to be thrown in. He went without offering the slightest resistance; but just as they reached the bank the muscular preacher turned nimbly, and bobbing up and down twice, in the twinkling of an eye, he flung into the creek first one, then the other of his would-be duckers. While this was going on another carriage was being rolled towards the water, about twenty yards away. This band was headed by the two Wagner boys, who, sufficiently intoxicated to be reckless of danger, were pulling the buggy by the shafts; but while they were pulling it in front others were pushing from behind, and when they came to the brink over went the buggy and the two brothers into the creek! Mingled shouts of victory and derision went up, and it was some time before the younger of the two got out of the water and climbed, half drowned, up the bank.

Several knock-down fights were going on in the vicinity, and amidst the general uproar no one had time to think of the lifeless body of the other brother, now lying in the creek.

Azariah James, Elder Johnson, Isaac Snedeker, and their assistants had given the ringleaders a severe drubbing, stripped them of their weapons and driven them, like so many sheep, in every direction.

Azariah James and Isaac Snedeker now formed a party to attack the vendors of whisky, which they did at the break of day, driving them from the place after pouring out the whisky on the ground.

Not a cloud was to be seen when the sun rose that Sunday morning. The smoke from the breakfast fires curled slowly up through the trees, and the odour of burning leaves and dry twigs perfumed the air with delicious fragrance. The day was warm; people felt it was good to be alive, and many expressed a wish that life would always be just like this.

Elihu Gest was right when he predicted that nothing much would come of the morning service. Serena Busby said the only two things the people did with spirit was eating and singing. Alone, of all the leaders in the camp, the Load-Bearer took a joyful view of the religious situation. The others were growing more and more pessimistic.

"The people air plumb sot in the sins o' the flesh," was what Elder Johnson said when he left the platform after the morning service; but Elihu Gest went so far as to whistle with "good feelin's," so that many of the preachers began to regard him as somewhat *suspect* in earnestness. The proceedings at the afternoon meeting were little more than a repetition of the preceding service; Elihu Gest, however, was nowhere to be seen and Uriah Busby guessed he was "away summars wrastlin' fer extry power."

The night settled down on the camp clear, calm, and beautiful; the people gathered in their places before the great platform and altar palings a full half-hour before the time fixed for the opening exercises, and the number present exceeded that of any meeting yet held.

However, services did not begin for some little time after the hour fixed, as the body of the drowned man was not discovered in the creek till now, and the preachers were engaged in consultation behind the big tent.

As the evening wore on the air became close and sultry, and a feeling of lethargy bore down on the people. Someone had advised the singing of several hymns as the best mode of getting the congregation into working order, and hymn after hymn was sung while a tall, long-haired leader stood beating time with his outstretched arm, waving to and fro with an eccentric lilt of the body, up and down. The platform was now filled with the preachers and exhorters, and in some manner the whole front and all the surrounding camp seemed metamorphosed. Something extraordinary had happened. Yet it was not possible to say what.

A storm was approaching; but those who were engaged in singing paid little heed to the rumbling of thunder. A few minutes more and a squall descended over the camp and a vivid flash sent a thrill through the assembly. The crash was followed by a hurricane of shifting light that swept down closer and closer over the camp. The lightning seemed to spring from the ground, the air, the woods, the camp itself, and it seemed as if objects moved in keeping with the quick sheets of fire that came as bolts from the heavens. Only a few lights were left in the lanterns, and there was something spectral about the vast concourse swaying like grizzled phantoms on the brink of a yawning abyss.

Just before the hurricane passed away a dazzling bolt struck the big elm beside the platform. It fell in a blue-white zigzag, and to many of the more superstitious it resembled nothing so much as a fiery serpent poured from a vial of wrath overhead, for it split the elm in two, the peal of thunder and the cleaving timber mingling in one terrific report.

A great shout arose from the people near the tree, and the commotion in that part of the meeting had hardly subsided when a voice was heard as one calling from the shores of Tartarus.

Elihu Gest stood on the platform facing the assembly, and a new meaning was added to the confusion and the ghostly candle-light. A picture of peculiar fascination was now presented to the wondering and half-dazed people. Arrayed behind the Load-Bearer, in a jagged semi-circle that stretched from one end of the platform to the other, sat all the preachers and exhorters. Witnesses who had once mourned as penitents before the altar now mar-shalled to make others mourn, as fixed and motionless as statues hewn from syenite; for there was about them something of the mien of Egyptian bas-reliefs seated at the door separating life and death. Some were bearded and grimly entrenched behind a hairy mask; others, in their long, pointed goatees, sharpened the picture; while others again, clean-shaven, and peering straight before them, presented a death-like pallor, at once frail and frightful, suggesting the keynote of the incommensurable symphony of human emotions now about to begin.

A deep, apprehensive solemnity pervaded every portion of the congregation when the Load-Bearer shouted, in tones that penetrated to the far end of the camp: "You are being weighed in the balance! Tophet is yawning for the unregenerate!"

A sensation as if the ground had begun to move and float spread through the multitude; and when, a little later, he cried: "You're hangin' to the hinges of Time by a hair!" all doubts vanished. Heads began to droop, bodies swayed from side to side, and then, one by one, in couples, in groups, everywhere in the meeting, people fell to the ground, while stifled groans and loud lamentations issued from hundreds of throats at once.

The mourners at the altar were now several rows deep, but still the crowd staggered forward. The camp resembled a coast strewn with the dead and dying after a great wreck, and a murmuring tumult alternately rose and fell like that from a moaning wind and a surging sea.

The night of nights had come! It seemed as if hundreds were in the throes of death and would never rise, so that a mingling of pity and dread filled those who had long since professed religion; for the strange union of material and spiritual forces, the upturned faces, the gaping mouths, the gasping sighs, the clenched hands, the sudden falling away of all wordly props, the swift descent from the mountain of vanity to the vale of sorrows rendered, for a moment, even the helpers and exhorters speechless; but, as Elihu Gest finished, the exhorters on the platform rose and scattered, each to a particular work, some descending amongst the people, some addressing them from the stand.

All the camp lights were now burning. In the midst of the greatest confusion Squire Higgins stood up where he could be seen, and called out: "Is Sister Kezia Jordan present?"

The people at that corner of the meeting rose from their seats. The Load-Bearer and Azariah James were lifting someone on to the corner of the platform. Again Squire Higgins stood up and called out Mrs. Jordan's name, and the word was passed from one end of the camp to the other. "Sister Jordan! where is Sister Jordan?" All preaching and exhorting ceased. An awful silence settled over the meeting, for there, on the platform, lay all that was left of Alek Jordan, who had been killed under the big elm when a portion of the tree had fallen.

At last Mrs. Jordan appeared at the bottom of the steps, at the left. She looked as if she might be walking in her sleep, and Martha Higgins was leading her by the arm. They mounted the steps slowly. At the top Elihu Gest and Azariah James stood waiting. On the platform a transformation had occurred. Seated again in a long semi-circle were the stern, statuesque figures, the faces more solemn and anxious, more strained and yearning than ever; and as Kezia Jordan passed along the platform and approached the remains the Load-Bearer turned as if suddenly inspired, and addressed her with the words: "The Lord giveth and the Lord taketh away," and all the preachers finished the sentence with him: "Blessed be the name of the Lord."

Mrs. Jordan now stood full in the lantern light, and her pallor was plainly visible. She bent over the body, then rose and whispered some words to Elihu Gest. He turned, and facing the multitude announced as loud as he could speak that Sister Jordan accepted this great affliction in a spirit of faith and resignation, and with her hand across her forehead, her eyes half-closed, like one who had been dazed by a sudden and bewildering vision, Kezia Jordan was led away by Martha Higgins and the Load-Bearer down the steps.

Prayers and exhortations followed, and the shouting, the hurrying to and fro, gave place to a feeling it would be impossible to describe.

And now, far down on the outskirts of the congregation, a voice was heard, high, shrill, and broken, which caused the people to turn in their seats and riveted every eye to a spot where a tall figure advanced, dimly visible, up the middle aisle. Out of the woods and the night the apparition seemed to have come, and with tottering steps, hair dishevelled, face trembling and distorted, the once unbending form of Minerva Wagner staggered towards the mourners' bench, the colour gone from her rugged face, the indomitable will from her proud, grey eyes, all her strength departed.

She had just left the body of her son.

"Take me, take me, in all my misery!" she cried out. "I'm an old woman in despair! I'm a stricken woman! Pray for me!"

She turned twice in a sort of whirl, and cast a look of unutterable woe on the people on either side, who, seized with feelings of awe and dismay at the sight before them, could scarcely realise what was happening. She staggered on, now assisted by friendly hands, and, when she arrived at the altar, fell in a swoon among the long rows of mourners.

All night the revival went on, and the next day, and the next; but on the same Sunday night, as the Load-Bearer left the camp grounds, and heard the multitude singing:

> "The year of jubilee has come,
>   Return ye ransomed sinners home"—

he waved his hand and cried: "Let 'em mourn, let 'em mourn; jedgment ain't far off!"

Prairie State Books

1988

Mr. Dooley in Peace and in War
FINLEY PETER DUNNE

Life in Prairie Land
ELIZA W. FARNHAM

Carl Sandburg
HARRY GOLDEN

The Sangamon
EDGAR LEE MASTERS

American Years
HAROLD SINCLAIR

The Jungle
UPTON SINCLAIR

1989

Twenty Years at Hull-House
JANE ADDAMS

They Broke the Prairie
EARNEST ELMO CALKINS

The Illinois
JAMES GRAY

The Valley of Shadows:
Sangamon Sketches
FRANCIS GRIERSON

The Precipice
ELIA W. PEATTIE